William Shakespeare's Hamlet: A Retelling in Prose

David Bruce

Published by David Bruce, 2022.

This is a work of fiction. Similarities to real people, places, or events are entirely coincidental.

WILLIAM SHAKESPEARE'S HAMLET: A RETELLING IN PROSE

First edition. July 24, 2022.

Copyright © 2022 David Bruce.

ISBN: 979-8201981143

Written by David Bruce.

Table of Contents

Dedication

Dedicated to Carl Eugene Bruce and Josephine Saturday Bruce

My father, Carl Eugene Bruce, died on 24 October 2013. He used to work for Ohio Power, and at one time, his job was to shut off the electricity of people who had not paid their bills. He sometimes would find a home with an impoverished mother and some children. Instead of shutting off their electricity, he would tell the mother that she needed to pay her bill or soon her electricity would be shut off. He would write on a form that no one was home when he stopped by because if no one was home he did not have to shut off their electricity.

The best good deed that anyone ever did for my father occurred after a storm that knocked down many power lines. He and other linemen worked long hours and got wet and cold. Their feet were freezing because water got into their boots and soaked their socks. Fortunately, a kind woman gave my father and the other linemen dry socks to wear.

My mother, Josephine Saturday Bruce, died on 14 June 2003. She used to work at a store that sold clothing. One day, an impoverished mother with a baby clothed in rags walked into the store and started shoplifting in an interesting way: The mother took the rags off her baby and dressed the infant in new clothing. My mother knew that this mother could not afford to buy the clothing, but she helped the mother dress her baby and then she watched as the mother walked out of the store without paying.

****

The doing of good deeds is important. As a free person, you can choose to live your life as a good person or as a bad person. To be a good person, do good deeds. To be a bad person, do bad deeds. If you do good deeds, you will become good. If you do bad deeds, you will become bad. To become the person you want to be, act as if you already are that kind of person. Each of us chooses what kind of person we will become. To become a good person, do the things a good person does. To become a bad person, do the things a bad person does. The opportunity to take action to become the kind of person you want to be is yours.

Human beings have free will. According to the Babylonian Niddah 16b, whenever a baby is to be conceived, the Lailah (angel in charge of

contraception) takes the drop of semen that will result in the conception and asks God, "Sovereign of the Universe, what is going to be the fate of this drop? Will it develop into a robust or into a weak person? An intelligent or a stupid person? A wealthy or a poor person?" The Lailah asks all these questions, but it does not ask, "Will it develop into a righteous or a wicked person?" The answer to that question lies in the decisions to be freely made by the human being that is the result of the conception.

A Buddhist monk visiting a class wrote this on the chalkboard: "EVERYONE WANTS TO SAVE THE WORLD, BUT NO ONE WANTS TO HELP MOM DO THE DISHES." The students laughed, but the monk then said, "Statistically, it's highly unlikely that any of you will ever have the opportunity to run into a burning orphanage and rescue an infant. But, in the smallest gesture of kindness — a warm smile, holding the door for the person behind you, shoveling the driveway of the elderly person next door — you have committed an act of immeasurable profundity, because to each of us, our life is our universe."

In her book titled *I Have Chosen to Stay and Fight*, comedian Margaret Cho writes, "I believe that we get complimentary snack-size portions of the afterlife, and we all receive them in a different way." For Ms. Cho, many of her snack-size portions of the afterlife come in hip hop music. Other people get different snack-size portions of the afterlife, and we all must be on the lookout for them when they come our way. And perhaps doing good deeds and experiencing good deeds are snack-size portions of the afterlife.

• The Zen master Gisan was taking a bath. The water was too hot, so he asked a student to add some cold water to the bath. The student brought a bucket of cold water, added some cold water to the bath, and then threw the rest of the water on a rocky path. Gisan scolded the student: "Everything can be used. Why did you waste the rest of the water by pouring it on the path? There are some plants nearby which could have used the water. What right do you have to waste even a drop of water?" The student became enlightened and changed his name to Tekisui, which means "Drop of Water."

Educate Yourself
Read Like A Wolf Eats
Be Excellent to Each Other
Books Then, Books Now, Books Forever

***

In this retelling, as in all my retellings, I have tried to make the work of literature accessible to modern readers who may lack some of the knowledge about mythology, religion, and history that the literary work's contemporary audience had.

Do you know a language other than English? If you do, I give you permission to translate this book, copyright your translation, publish or self-publish it, and keep all the royalties for yourself. (Do give me credit, of course, for the original retelling.)

I would like to see my retellings of classic literature used in schools, so I give permission to the country of Finland (and all other countries) to give copies of this book to all students forever. I also give permission to the state of Texas (and all other states) to give copies of this book to all students forever. I also give permission to all teachers to give copies of this book to all students forever.

Teachers need not actually teach my retellings. Teachers are welcome to give students copies of my eBooks as background material. For example, if they are teaching Homer's *Iliad* and *Odyssey*, teachers are welcome to give students copies of my *Virgil's* Aeneid: *A Retelling in Prose* and tell students, "Here's another ancient epic you may want to read in your spare time."

CAST OF CHARACTERS

MALE CHARACTERS

GHOST of Hamlet's father.

CLAUDIUS, King of Denmark.

HAMLET, Prince, son to the late King Hamlet, and nephew to the present King Claudius. Queen Gertrude is his mother.

POLONIUS, counselor to the King. Polonius is old, and his children are Ophelia and Laertes.

HORATIO, friend to Hamlet. Attended University of Wittenberg with Hamlet.

LAERTES, son to Polonius.

VOLTEMAND, CORNELIUS, Danish ambassadors sent to Norway.

ROSENCRANTZ, GUILDENSTERN, childhood friends to Hamlet.

OSRIC, a foolish courtier.

A Gentleman.

A Priest.

MARCELLUS, BARNARDO, officers.

FRANCISCO, a soldier.

REYNALDO, servant to Polonius.

Players (actors).

First Player, acts the part of the King.
Second Player, acts the part of the Queen.
Third Player, acts the part of the King's nephew, Lucianus.
Fourth Player, speaks the Prologue.

Two Clowns, gravediggers.

FORTINBRAS, Prince of Norway.

A Captain.

English Ambassadors.

FEMALE CHARACTERS

GERTRUDE, Queen of Denmark, and mother to Hamlet.

OPHELIA, daughter to Polonius.

MINOR CHARACTERS
Lords, Ladies, Officers, Soldiers, Sailors, Messengers, and other Attendants.
SCENE
Elsinore in Denmark, the royal castle and its surroundings.

CHAPTER 1
— 1.1 —

At a guard post of the King of Denmark's castle at Elsinore, Francisco stood guard. The time was midnight, and the weather was cold.

Barnardo walked over to Francisco and asked, "Who's there?"

Francisco replied, "No, *you* answer *me*. I am the sentinel. Stand still, and identify yourself."

"Long live the King!" Barnardo replied. This was enough to show that he was a friend and not an enemy.

"Are you Barnardo?" Francisco asked.

"I am he."

"You have come very promptly at your appointed time to relieve me."

"The bell just now struck twelve," Barnardo said. "Go to bed, Francisco."

"For this relief, much thanks. It is bitterly cold, and I am sick at heart."

"Have you had a quiet guard?"

"Not even a mouse is stirring."

"Well, good night. If you meet Horatio and Marcellus, the partners of my watch, tell them to come quickly."

"I think I hear them," Francisco said. "Stop! Who's there?"

Horatio and Marcellus walked over to the two guards.

Horatio, who was a friend to Prince Hamlet, answered Francisco's question: "Friends to this country."

Marcellus added, "And loyal liegemen to the King of Denmark."

"May God give you a good night," Francisco said.

"Farewell, honest soldier," Marcellus said, and then he asked, "Who has relieved you?"

"Barnardo is taking my place. May God give you a good night."

Francisco departed.

Marcellus called, "Hey! Barnardo!"

Barnardo replied, "Hello. Is Horatio there?"

Horatio replied, "Here is a piece of him," and then he stuck out his hand to shake hands with Barnardo.

"Welcome, Horatio," Barnardo said. "Welcome, good Marcellus."

"Has this thing appeared again tonight?" Marcellus asked.

"I have seen nothing."

"Horatio says it is only our fantasy," Marcellus said. "He will not believe that this dreaded sight, which we have seen twice, is real. Therefore, I have entreated him to come along with us to watch all through this night. That way, if this apparition comes again, he may see it with his own eyes and speak to it."

"Tush, tush," Horatio said. "It will not appear."

"Sit down awhile," Barnardo replied, "and let us once again assail your ears, which are so fortified against and disbelieving of our story about what we have seen during two nights."

"Well, let us sit down," Horatio said, "and let us hear Barnardo tell his story."

"Last night, when the yonder same star that's west of the Pole Star had made its course to illuminate that part of the night sky where now it burns, Marcellus and I, the bell then striking one — "

The ghost walked onto the scene.

"Quiet! Stop talking!" Marcellus said. "Look there! Here it comes again!"

"The ghost has the same shape it had," Barnardo said. "It looks exactly like King Hamlet, the King who is dead."

"You are a scholar," Marcellus said. "Speak to it, Horatio."

As a scholar, Horatio knew the proper Latin words to use to ward off the ghost if it turned out to be malevolent.

"Doesn't it look like the late King?" Barnardo asked. "Look at it closely, Horatio."

"It looks very much like the late King," Horatio said. "This sight harrows me with fear and wonder. It is as if my skin were being raked with a harrow."

"The ghost wants to be spoken to," Barnardo said.

Ghosts cannot speak until after they are spoken to.

"Question it, Horatio," Marcellus said.

Horatio asked the ghost, "What are you that is usurping this time of night, and is usurping that fair and warlike form in which the majesty of the buried King of Denmark did sometimes march? By Heaven, I order you to speak!"

Marcellus said, "The ghost is offended and does not speak."

"Look!" Barnardo said. "It is stalking away!"

"Stay!" Horatio shouted. "Speak, speak! I order you to speak!"

The ghost stalked out of sight.

"It is gone," Marcellus said, "and it will not answer you."

"What now, Horatio!" Barnardo said. "You tremble and look pale. Isn't this something more than fantasy? What do you think about it?"

"Before my God, I would not believe this without my having seen it with the sensible and true evidence of my own eyes," Horatio said.

"Didn't it resemble the late King Hamlet?" Marcellus asked.

"It resembles the late King just as much as you resemble yourself," Horatio replied. "The ghost was wearing the very same armor that the late King was wearing when he combatted the ambitious King of Norway. The ghost frowned exactly the same way the late King frowned when once, in an angry and physical argument, he smote the Polish soldiers who were crossing the ice on their sleds. It is strange."

"Twice before, and exactly at this dead, dark, and dreary hour," Marcellus said, "the ghost has walked with a martial stride during our watch."

"I do not know what exactly to think," Horatio said, "but in general my opinion is that this ghost is a sign of some strange and violent disturbance coming to our state."

"Please, sit down, and tell me, he who knows," Marcellus said, "why each night the citizens of our country toil in a strict and most observant watch. Also tell me why bronze cannon are cast each day and why implements of war are being purchased in foreign marketplaces. Why have shipwrights been drafted to do their work every day with no Sabbath as a day of rest? What is the meaning of all this? What is so important that this sweaty haste results in such work being done both during the night and during the day? Who can tell me this?"

"I can," Horatio replied. "Our last King, the late King Hamlet, whose image just now appeared to us, was, as you know, by Fortinbras of Norway and his competitive pride challenged to a combat. Our valiant King Hamlet — this side of our known world knew him to be valiant — slew this Fortinbras in that combat.

"By a sealed and legal agreement, well ratified by law and the code of heraldry, Fortinbras forfeited, with his life, all the lands that he personally possessed to the conqueror.

"Our King Hamlet had likewise risked some of his personally owned lands, enough to equal the amount of land waged by Fortinbras. If Fortinbras had defeated and killed King Hamlet, Fortinbras would have acquired those lands. Instead, King Hamlet defeated and killed Fortinbras, thereby acquiring the lands that Fortinbras had wagered. All of this was in accordance to the legal contract that the two men had made.

"King Hamlet died and left those lands he had won to his son, Prince Hamlet. Old Fortinbras had wagered all his lands, and so he had no lands to leave to his son, young Fortinbras.

"Now, sir, young Fortinbras, who is hot and full of undisciplined and unrestrained mettle, has in the outskirts of Norway here and there sharked up a list of lawless reprobates, indiscriminately adding them to his army the way that a shark indiscriminately adds fish to its belly. These landless and lawless reprobates will serve as the food that propels some enterprise that has a stomach in it — the enterprise needs these soldiers the way that a stomach needs food.

"That enterprise is no other than — as is well evident to our country — to take from us, by force and compulsion, those lands lost by his father, the elder Fortinbras.

"This, I take it, is the main reason for our preparations, the cause of this our watch and the fountainhead of this furious activity and turmoil in the land."

"I think that what you have said is correct," Barnardo said. "It is appropriate that this portentous figure — this ghost — comes armed during our watch; the ghost is very much like the late King who was and is the cause of these wars."

"This sight of the ghost troubles the mind's eye," Horatio said. "In the most high and flourishing state of Rome, a little before the very mighty Julius Caesar fell, the graves stood open without their tenants and the dead, wrapped in sheets, squeaked and gibbered in the Roman streets. They were deadly portents just like meteors that trail trains of fire, dews of blood, and threatening signs in the Sun. In addition, the Moon, that moist planet that has power over the empire of Neptune, Roman King of the Seas, because it controls the tides, was almost completely blotted out because of an eclipse — it seemed as if it were the Day of Judgment.

"These same portents that foretold the assassination of Julius Caesar, these same portents that are precursors of fierce events, these same portents that are harbingers that always precede calamities and are prologue to a coming disaster

— Heaven and Earth have joined together to show these same portents to Denmark and to the Danes."

Horatio looked up and said, "But wait — look! Look, the ghost is coming here again!"

The ghost stalked closer to the three men.

"I'll cross its path even though it blasts and destroys me," Horatio said.

He said to the ghost, "Stay, illusion! If you can make any sound, if you can use your voice, speak to me. If I can do any good thing that will bring ease to you and honor to me, speak to me."

The ghost opened its mouth, but a rooster — aka a cock — crowed.

Horatio continued, "If you have knowledge about evil coming to your country, which, perhaps, foreknowing may allow us to avoid, ghost, speak! Or if you have buried during your life ill-begotten treasure in the womb of the Earth, for which, they say, you spirits often walk in death, tell us about it."

The ghost moved away, and Horatio called, "Stay, and speak!"

The ghost ignored Horatio, who then said, "Stop it, Marcellus."

"Shall I strike at it with my pike?" Marcellus asked.

"Yes, if it will not stand still."

Looking in one direction, Barnardo said, "It is here!"

Looking in another direction, Horatio said, "It is here!"

Marcellus said, "It is gone!"

The ghost could not be seen.

Marcellus added, "We do it wrong when we act so majestically and imperiously and threaten it with a show of violence. After all, the ghost is as invulnerable as the air and when we strike at it with our pikes we do it no harm. The ghost mocks our vain blows and maliciousness."

"It was about to speak, but the cock crowed," Barnardo said.

"And then it started like a guilty thing hearing a fearful summons," Horatio said. "I have heard that the cock, which is the trumpeter to the morning, does with his lofty and shrill-sounding throat awaken Phoebus Apollo, the god of day. Hearing the cock's warning, any spirit that is wandering out of its boundary hurries back to its place of confinement, whether in sea or fire, or in earth or air. What we have just witnessed is evidence that what I have heard is true."

"The ghost faded when the cock crowed," Marcellus said. "Some say that when that season comes in which the birth of our Savior is celebrated, the bird of dawning — the cock — sings, aka crows, all night long. And then, they say, no spirit dares to stir abroad. The nights are wholesome. No planets exert an evil influence, no fairy casts a spell, and no witch has the power to charm — because Christmas is so sanctified and gracious a time."

"So I have heard and I do in part believe it," Horatio said. "But, look, the morning, clad in a russet-colored mantle, walks over the dew of yonder high hill in the East. Let us end our watch. I advise that we tell what we have seen tonight to young Prince Hamlet. I believe, upon my life, that this spirit, which will not speak to us, will speak to him.

"What do you think? Do you agree that we should inform him about it? Do you agree that our friendship to Hamlet and our duty make it necessary for us to tell Hamlet what we have seen?"

"You are right," Marcellus said. "Let us tell Hamlet what we have seen, please. I know where we can easily find him this morning."

In a room of state in the castle were King Claudius, Queen Gertrude, Hamlet, Polonius, Laertes (Polonius' son), Voltemand, and Cornelius. Also present were other lords and some servants. Hamlet was dressed in black, the color of mourning.

Using the royal plural, King Claudius said, "Although the memory of the death of King Hamlet, our dear brother, is still green and fresh, and although it was fitting for us to bear our hearts in grief and for our whole Kingdom to be knit together in one brow of woe, yet discretion has so far fought with nature that we with wisest sorrow think about the late King Hamlet and at the same time remember our own position in the living world. Therefore, our former sister-in-law have we, as if with a defeated joy — with one eye smiling and the other eye dripping tears of sadness, with mirth at a funeral and with dirge at a marriage, with delight and dole weighing equally — married and taken as our wife, and no one has objected to our marriage. Our former sister-in-law is now our Queen, the imperial female sharer of the crown of this nation preparing for war. We have not gone against your very mature wisdom, which has freely approved this marriage all along. To all of you, we give our thanks.

"Now we must talk about young Fortinbras, who holds our worth in little regard, or who thinks that because of the death of our dear brother, the late King Hamlet, our nation is disturbed and is in disorder. These mistaken thoughts of his are allied with his dream of gaining personal advantages by threatening Denmark. Young Fortinbras has not failed to pester us with messages that demand the surrender of those lands that were lost by his father, in accordance with the law, to our most valiant brother. So much for what he is demanding: All this you know.

"Now for new information concerning what we ourself have decided — that is the main purpose and business of this meeting. We have here written a letter to the King of Norway, who is the uncle of young Fortinbras. His uncle became King of Norway after his father, the elder Fortinbras, died. Powerless and bedridden, the current King of Norway scarcely hears about his nephew's intentions and actions — I have written him to ask that he stop young Fortinbras from proceeding further in this business. The King of Norway has the power to do that because the levies of soldiers — everyone who has joined young Fortinbras — are citizens of Norway and therefore subject to his rule. We now send you, good Cornelius, and you, Voltemand, as bearers of this greeting and as ambassadors to the aged King of Norway; we give to you no further personal power to do business with the King of Norway. You can do no more than the scope that these detailed documents allow. Farewell, and show your duty to me in your speed in accomplishing this task. We need not hear a long and flowery address of etiquette."

"In delivering these documents and in all other things, we will show our duty," Cornelius and Voltemand said together.

"We do not doubt it," King Claudius said. "Heartily we say farewell to you."

Cornelius and Voltemand departed.

King Claudius continued, "And now, Laertes, what's the news with you? You told us that you had some request to make of us; what is it, Laertes? You cannot speak of anything reasonable to the King of Denmark, and waste your words. What can you reasonably request, Laertes, that shall not be my gift rather than your request? The head is not more closely related to the heart, the hand is not more instrumental to the mouth, than is the throne of Denmark to your father. We — the entire monarchy and ourself — value your father highly. What would you like to have, Laertes?"

"My dread lord," Laertes said, "I request your leave and permission for me to return to France. From there willingly I came to Denmark to do my duty and be present at your coronation, yet now that this duty is done, I must confess that my thoughts and wishes bend again toward France and I hope that you will grant me permission to return there."

"Have you your father's permission?" King Claudius asked.

He then asked, "Polonius, what do you say about this?"

"He has, my lord, made laborious petitions to wring from me my slow permission for him to return to France. Finally, I gave him my consent. I stamped my seal of approval upon his request. I ask you, therefore, to allow him to go."

"Take your fair hour, Laertes," King Claudius said. "Let your time of youth be yours to spend as you will in accordance with your best qualities. You have our permission to return to France."

He then said, "But now, my nephew Hamlet, who is also my son —"

Hamlet thought, *A little more than kin, and less than kind. In other words: The nearer in kin, the less in kindness. And in yet other words: The closer the relationship, the greater the dislike. Am I your son? I say no. To call me your son is more than our actual relationship will allow. I do not accept you as my father. I also do not regard you as kind in the sense of being benevolent. The word "kind" also refers to the natural quality of family members; they should be united in a community of love toward each other. You and I do not have that. You married my mother, who is your brother's widow; I do not consider such a marriage natural — it is incestuous.*

"How is it that the clouds still hang on you?" King Claudius asked Hamlet.

"That is not true," Hamlet replied. "I am too much in the Sun."

He thought, *And I do not like being called your son.*

Queen Gertrude, Hamlet's mother, said, "Good Hamlet, take off and put away your night-colored clothing, and let your eye look like a friend on the King of Denmark. Do not forever with your downcast eyes seek for your noble father in the dust. You know that everything that lives must die, passing through nature to eternity."

"Yes, that is a universal truth," Hamlet said.

"If you know that, why does it seem that you are having such a hard time accepting your father's death?"

"Madam, 'seem'?" Hamlet replied. "I really am having such a hard time accepting my father's death. The word 'seem' does not apply to me. It is not alone my inky-black cloak, good mother, nor the customary and conventional suits of solemn black, nor the windy sighs of forced breath, no, nor the fruitful river of tears flowing from the eyes, nor the dejected expression of the visage, together with all forms, moods, shapes of grief, that can denote me truly. All of these indeed seem; they can be appearances of something that is not truly felt. They are actions that a man might act out hypocritically, but I have that within myself that surpasses show and goes beyond appearances. These other things are only the trappings and the suits of woe."

"It is sweet and commendable in your nature, Hamlet, to give these mourning duties to your father," King Claudius said. "But, you must know that your father lost his father. That father also lost his father. With the loss of each father, the survivor is bound in filial obligation to do as the funeral services demand and to grieve for some time. However, to persevere in obstinate sorrow is a course of impious stubbornness; it is unmanly grief. It shows a will most incorrect and in opposition to Heaven, a heart unsupported by religious belief, a mind lacking the virtue of patience, an understanding ignorant and uneducated. When we know that something must occur and is in fact as common as the most ordinary thing that we can sense, why should we in our peevish opposition take it to heart and mourn it excessively? Ha! It is a transgression and sin against Heaven, a transgression and sin against the dead, a transgression and sin against nature, and a most absurd and sinful transgression against reason, whose common theme is the death of fathers. Everyone who has witnessed death in the first corpse to the corpse of the person who died today has cried, 'This must be so.'"

The first corpse was a murder victim. Cain killed Abel, his brother. This story is recounted in Genesis 4:8.

King Claudius continued, "We ask you to please throw to earth this unprevailing sorrow — it can gain nothing — and think of us as of a father. Let the world take note that you are the most immediate to our throne. Denmark is an elective monarchy, but we now use our voice to say that we want you to succeed us on the throne. I feel the love for you that a biological father bears his son.

"We know that you want to go back to school in Wittenberg, but that is in opposition to what we desire. And so we beseech you to change your mind and remain here, in the cheer and comfort of our eye. You are our most important courtier, our kinsman, and our son."

Queen Gertrude said, "Please do what I want you to do, Hamlet. Please stay here and do not return to Wittenberg."

"I shall to the best of my ability obey you, madam," Hamlet replied.

"Why, that is a loving and a fair reply," King Claudius said. "Be a member of the royal family and stay here in Denmark."

He said to Queen Gertrude, "Madam, come. This gentle and unforced accord of Hamlet to our wishes sits smiling in my heart. To celebrate this, each time that we, the King of Denmark, will take a drink today, the great cannon will fire into the clouds, and the Heavens will all bruit and spread the King's toast again, re-speaking it with Earthly thunder. Come, let's go now."

Everyone except Hamlet left the room.

Hamlet said to himself, "Oh, I wish that this too, too solid flesh would melt, thaw, and resolve itself into a dew! Would that my body would waste away on its own! Or I wish that the Everlasting had not fixed His canon — his eternal law — against self-slaughter! Exodus 20:13 states, '*Thou shalt not kill*,' and that includes a prohibition against killing oneself. Oh, God! God! How weary, stale, flat, and unprofitable seems to me the entire business of this world! Ha! This world is an unweeded garden, which goes to seed; things rank and gross in nature entirely possess it. That it should come to this!

"My father is only two months dead — no, not so much, not even two months. My father was so excellent a King; he was, compared to this King Claudius, Hyperion the god of the Sun compared to a lustful half-man, half-goat satyr. My father was so loving to my mother that he would not allow the winds of Heaven to blow against her face too roughly. Heaven and Earth, must I remember! Why, my mother would hang on my father, as if increase of affection had grown by what it fed on: and yet, within a month — let me not think about it! Frailty, your name is woman! She wore new shoes when she followed my father's body as it went to the tomb. She cried like Niobe, who wept after all of her sons and all of her daughters died in a single day. A little, short month later, before those shoes were old, she married my uncle — oh, God, even a beast that lacks the ability to reason would have mourned longer!

"My mother married my uncle. He is my father's brother, but he is no more like my father than I am like the super-strong Hercules. She married my uncle within a month of my father's death. Even before the salt of very unrighteous tears had left the red flush of her bitter eyes, she married him. Oh, most wicked speed, to hasten with such dexterity and jump into incestuous sheets! It is not good, and it cannot come to be good. But break, my heart, because I must hold my tongue."

Horatio, Marcellus, and Barnardo walked over to Hamlet.

Horatio greeted Hamlet: "Hail to your lordship!"

"I am glad to see you well," Hamlet said. "You are Horatio, if I am not mistaken."

"I am Horatio, my lord, and I am your poor servant ever."

"Sir, my good friend, I'll change that name with you," Hamlet said.

He meant that he would change the name "servant" to the name "friend." John 15:15 states, "*Henceforth call I you not servants: for the servant knoweth*

Or, possibly, he meant that he would exchange names with Horatio — he would be Horatio's servant.

Either way, Hamlet and Horatio were friends.

Hamlet added, "And what brings you here from Wittenberg, Horatio?"

He then noticed Marcellus and greeted him, "Marcellus!"

Marcellus replied, "My good lord."

Hamlet said, "I am very glad to see you. Good day, sir."

He then again asked Horatio, "What brings you here from Wittenberg?"

"A truant disposition, my good lord," Horatio replied.

"I would not hear your enemy say that about you," Hamlet said, "and I will not allow you to do my ear the violence that would make it trust your own report against yourself. I know that you are no truant. But what is your business here in Elsinore? We'll teach you to drink deep before you depart. Danes are famous for their deep drinking."

"My lord, I came to see your father's funeral," Horatio replied.

"Please, do not mock me, fellow student," Hamlet said. "I think your purpose in coming here was to see my mother's wedding."

"Indeed, my lord, the marriage quickly followed the funeral."

"Thrift, thrift, Horatio!" Hamlet said. "The hot baked meat pies for the funeral feast were set down cold on the tables for the marriage feast. I would prefer to have seen my worst enemy in Heaven before I had seen that day, Horatio! My father! I think I see my father!"

Startled, and thinking of the ghost, Horatio said, "Where, my lord?"

"In my mind's eye, Horatio."

"I saw him some time ago," Horatio said. "He was a good-looking King."

"He was a man — the ideal of man; he was perfect in every way," Hamlet said. "I shall not look upon his like again."

"My lord, I think I saw him last night," Horatio said.

"Saw? Whom?"

"My lord, I think I saw the King your father."

"The King my father!"

"Control your wonderment for a while," Horatio said. "Listen with attentive ears until I can tell you what a marvelous thing I have seen with these gentlemen as witnesses."

"For God's love, let me hear," Hamlet said.

"These gentlemen, Marcellus and Barnardo, had twice on their watch, in the dead vast and middle of the night, encountered something strange. A figure like your father, armed exactly like him from top to toe, appeared before them, and with solemn march stalked slowly and stately by them. Three times he walked by their troubled and fear-surprised eyes, as close as the length of his truncheon. They, melted almost to jelly because of their fear, stood silently and did not dare to speak to him. This they fearfully and secretly told me, and I kept the watch with them the third night. Exactly as they had said, at the time they had stated and dressed the way that they had described, the apparition appeared. Each word they had spoken proved to be true and good. I was acquainted with your father. My hands are not more similar than was the apparition to your father."

"But where did this happen?" Hamlet asked.

"My lord, this happened upon the platform — the platform where the guns of the fort are mounted. That is where we kept our watch," Marcellus replied.

"Didn't you speak to the ghost?" Hamlet asked.

"My lord, I did," Horatio replied, "but it did not answer me. Once I thought that it lifted its head up and looked as if it were about to speak, but just then the cock crew loudly to announce the morning, and at the sound of the cock it shrunk hastily away and vanished from our sight."

"It is very strange."

"As I live, my honored lord, it is true, and we thought that it was our duty to let you know about it," Horatio said.

"Indeed, indeed, sirs, but this troubles me," Hamlet replied.

He asked Marcellus and Barnardo, "Do you have the watch tonight?"

"We do, my lord," they replied.

"Was the ghost armed?" Hamlet asked.

"It was armed, my lord," they replied. "It was wearing armor."

"From top to toe?"

"My lord, from head to foot," they replied.

"Then you did not see his face?"

"My lord, we did see the ghost's face," Horatio said, "The face guard of its helmet was up."

"How did he look?" Hamlet asked. "Did he frown and look fierce, like a warrior?"

"His countenance was more sorrowful than angry," Horatio replied.

"Was his face pale or a healthy red?"

"Very pale."

"And he fixed his eyes upon you?" Hamlet asked.

"Most constantly," Horatio said.

"I wish I had been there."

"It would have much amazed you."

"Very likely, very likely," Hamlet said. "Did it stay long?"

"As long as someone with moderate haste might count to a hundred," Horatio replied.

"Longer, longer," Marcellus and Barnardo objected.

"Not when I saw it," Horatio said.

"His beard was grizzled, wasn't it?" Hamlet asked.

"It was, as I have seen it in his life," Horatio said, "a sable silvered. His beard was black but streaked with white."

"I will watch with you tonight," Hamlet said. "Perhaps it will walk again."

"I predict it will," Horatio said.

"If it assumes my noble father's person, I'll speak to it, even if Hell itself should gape and order me to be silent," Hamlet said. "Please, if you have not already told someone what you saw, continue to keep what you saw secret. Whatever you see happen tonight, look at it closely but do not talk about it. I will reward your friendship. And so, farewell. Upon the guard platform, between eleven and twelve tonight, I'll visit you."

"We will do our duty to your honor," they replied.

"Give me your friendship, as I give you mine," Hamlet said. "Farewell."

Everyone except Hamlet departed.

Hamlet said to himself, "My father's spirit dressed in armor! All is not well; I suspect some foul play that the ghost wishes to inform me about. I wish that it were night! Until then, my soul, sit still. Foul deeds will rise, although all the Earth overwhelm them, to men's eyes. No matter how people try to hide foul deeds, they will become unhidden."

Laertes and Ophelia were in a room of Polonius' house. Laertes was preparing to return to France, and they were saying their goodbyes to each other.

"My luggage is on board ship," Laertes said. "Farewell. And, sister, if the winds are blowing in the right direction and a ship is ready to sail to France, do not sleep but instead write and send a letter to me."

"Can you doubt that I will write to you?" Ophelia asked.

"As for Hamlet and his trifling flirting with you, know that it is a temporary liking and a passing fancy and a youthful amorous sport. It is a violet in the springtime of youthful nature. It is an early flowering; it is not permanent. It is sweet, but it is not lasting. It is the perfume and pastime of a minute. Hamlet's feeling for you is no more than that."

"No more than that?" Ophelia asked.

"Think that it is no more than that," Laertes said. "As we grow, we do not grow only in physical size and strength of our temple the body, but we also grow in our mind and soul — our inward nature also grows and expands. Perhaps he loves you now, and now no stain or deceit does besmirch the honorableness of his will, but you must be aware and fear that because he is a great and important person his will is not his own. He himself is subject to his birth and rank, and so he cannot do as other, lesser people do. He may not, as unvalued and unimportant persons do, choose for himself whom to marry because the safety and health of this whole state of Denmark depend on his choice, and therefore his choice must be circumscribed — his choice must meet the approval of that body of citizens of whom he is the head.

"Therefore, if he says he loves you, you will be wise to believe it only to the extent that a man in his particular position can act on what he says, which is only as far as the general approval of the important citizens of Denmark will allow him to act.

"So weigh what loss your honor may sustain, if you listen to his songs of love with too credulous and believing ears. Weigh what loss your honor may sustain if you lose your heart to him, or if you open your chaste treasure — your virginity — to his uncontrolled demands.

"Fear it, Ophelia, fear it, my dear sister, and keep yourself in the rear of your affection, out of the shot and danger of desire. Don't display your affection, and so keep yourself safe. The most modest maiden is prodigal enough, if she unmasks her beauty to the Moon; she ought not to unmask her beauty to someone who will take advantage of her.

"The mere fact of virtue itself is not enough to escape malicious and destructive gossip. The cankerworm injures the young flowers of the spring very often before their buds have been disclosed, and in the morning and liquid dew of youth contagious infections are most imminent. Youth is a time of great promise — and great danger.

"Be wary therefore. The best safety lies in fear of danger. If you are not afraid of danger, you are not wary of danger, and so you can fall into danger. Youth often acts contrary to its better nature even when no temptation is near."

"I shall keep the content of this good lesson in and as a watchman for my heart," Ophelia replied, "but, my good brother, do not do as some pastors who lack grace do: They show me the steep and thorny way to Heaven, while like reckless libertines puffed up with pride, they tread the primrose path of wanton amusement — they do not take their own advice."

"Don't worry about me," Laertes said, adding, "I have stayed too long."

He heard a noise, looked up, and said, "Our father is coming."

Polonius entered the room, and Laertes said, "A double blessing is a double grace; occasion smiles upon a second leave. I get to have two farewells from my father."

"Are you still here, Laertes?" Polonius said. "For shame! The wind is blowing in the sails of your ship, and everyone is waiting for you!

"Well, take my blessing and my advice with you. Listen to what I have to say to you and engrave my words in your heart.

"Do not needlessly broadcast your thoughts, and do not act on any reckless thought.

"Be friendly, but do not be overly friendly. You need not be familiar with everybody.

"When you have friends who have proven themselves to be true throughout trials, keep them close to your soul with hoops of steel, but do not shake hands with every new and untested young man you meet.

"Beware of being involved in a quarrel, but once you are in the quarrel, act in such a way that the person arguing with you regrets it.

"Listen to every man, but give few men your recommendation.

"Listen to every man's opinion, but reserve your judgment and form your own opinions carefully.

"Buy as good clothing as you can afford, but do not buy clothing with fancy trimmings. You need to buy rich — not gaudy — clothing. What a man wears often reveals what a man is. In France, people of the best rank and station know and practice this wisdom — they have good taste in clothing.

"Neither a borrower nor a lender be, because when you make a loan, you often lose both your money and your friend, and if you borrow money you do not practice the virtue of thrift.

"Practice this above all: To your own self be true. If you do this, it must follow, as the night follows the day, that you cannot then be false to any man.

"Farewell, and may my blessing help you to practice what I have said!"

"Most humbly do I take my leave, my lord," Laertes said to his father.

"It is time for you to go," Polonius said. "Your servants are waiting for you."

"Farewell, Ophelia," Laertes said, "and remember well what I have said to you."

"Your words are locked in my memory, and you have the key. I will remember your words until you give me permission to forget them."

"Farewell," Laertes said, and then he departed.

"What is it, Ophelia, that Laertes has said to you?" Polonius asked.

"If it pleases you, he told me something concerning Lord Hamlet."

"This makes me remember something," Polonius said. "I have been told that Hamlet has very often recently spent private time with you, and that you yourself have been most free and bounteous of your time and have spent it with Hamlet. If what I have heard is true, and I have been told these things as a warning to be careful and protective of you, I must tell you that you are not acting in such a way that my daughter ought to act — you must protect your honor. What is going on between you and Hamlet? Tell me the truth."

"He has, my lord, of late made many tenders of his affection to me. He has let me know that he is fond of me."

The word "tender" means "offer." The word can mean "an offer of love," which is how Ophelia is using it, or it can mean "an offer of money," which is one of the ways Polonius will use it. The word "tender" can also refer to offers of other things.

"Affection! Ha! You speak like a green and inexperienced girl who is untried in such perilous circumstances. Do you believe his tenders of affection, as you call them?"

"I do not know, my lord, what I should think."

"By the Virgin Mary, I'll teach you what to think. Think of yourself as a baby who has mistaken these tenders for true pay, but these tenders are counterfeit — they are not sterling. Tender yourself more dearly — take better care of yourself. If you do not — and here I think I am overusing the word 'tender' — you'll tender me a fool."

By "tender me a fool," Polonius meant three things: 1) Ophelia will make a fool of herself, 2) Ophelia will make Polonius look like a fool, and 3) Ophelia will present Polonius with a fool — a bastard grandchild.

"My lord, he has made me his tenders of love in an honorable fashion."

"Aye, 'fashion' you may call it," Polonius said. "Ha!"

"And Hamlet has given confirmation of his tenders of love to me, my lord, with almost all the holy vows of Heaven."

"Hamlet's words are traps to catch woodcocks, which are very stupid birds. I know how the soul, when the blood burns, gives with careless generosity such vows of love to the tongue. These flares, daughter, give more light than heat, but both light and heat are as quickly extinguished as they are made. You must not mistake these quickly ending flares for real fire and real love.

"From this time on, do not spend so much time with Hamlet. Keep your maidenly presence away from him. You are the protectress of a treasure — your virginity — and you need not enter into negotiations for it just because a besieger wants you to.

"As for Lord Hamlet, remember that he is young and he has much more freedom to do what he wants than you do. In short, Ophelia, do not believe the vows that Hamlet makes to you. His vows of love are brokers who dress in holy vestments but who act as panderers to entice you into unholy acts of sin.

"This is all I have to say. From this time forth, I do not want you, in plain words, to misuse any of your free time by spending it in conversation with Lord Hamlet. Make sure that you do what I am telling you to do. Come along with me now."

"I shall obey you, my lord," Ophelia said to her father.

On the platform where the guards performed their duty, Hamlet, Horatio, and Marcellus stood.

"The air bites sharply," Hamlet said. "It is very cold."

"It is a nipping and sharp air," Horatio agreed.

"What time is it now?" Hamlet asked.

"I think that it is not yet midnight," Horatio replied.

"No, the bell struck twelve," Marcellus said.

"Really?" Horatio said. "I did not hear it. It is drawing near the time that the ghost is accustomed to walk."

Trumpets sounded, and cannons fired.

"What does this noise mean, my lord?" Horatio asked Hamlet.

"King Claudius stays awake tonight in order to carouse. He drinks many toasts, and he dances swaggering dances. As he drains his draughts of Rhine wine, the kettledrum and trumpet thus bray out the triumph of his pledge. The kettledrum and trumpet are signals to fire the cannon."

"Is this a Danish custom?" Horatio asked.

"Yes, indeed it is," Hamlet said, "but in my opinion, although I am a native of Denmark and to the manner born, it is a custom that would be more honorable in being breached than in being observed. This heavy-headed reveling with its drunken practitioners makes other nations both in the East and in the West criticize and censure us. They call us drunkards, and they stain our names and titles by calling us swine. These drunken revels take away from our achievements, even those that are worthiest of the greatest praise. They cause us to lose the best and most valuable part of our national character.

"It often happens in particular men that they have some vicious defect of nature. This defect may, for example, be present from their birth because of their heredity — wherein they are not guilty, since no one can choose his origin. They are born with an unbalanced personality that often breaks down the fences and forts of reason. Or they may develop a personality flaw or a bad habit that excessively influences and perverts what would be their decent behavior.

"As I say, these certain men are contaminated by one flaw of the personality, whether it comes from nature or from nurture or from the workings of fate. Although in everything else they are completely virtuous and completely pure in grace — as complete as it is possible for a living man to be — yet the general opinion of everybody focuses on that one fault. A very small amount of evil can throw a shadow over all his many good qualities and hurt his reputation."

Horatio said suddenly, "Look, my lord! Here comes the ghost!"

The ghost approached the men.

"May angels and ministers of grace defend us!" Hamlet said.

He said to the ghost, "You may be a spirit of health, an angel — or a damned goblin, a demon. You may bring with you airs from Heaven or blasts from Hell. Your intentions may be wicked or they may be charitable. But you have come here in such a shape as invites questioning, and so I shall speak to you. Because of the shape you have assumed, I will call you names that I hope will inspire you to speak to me. I will call you Hamlet, King, father, royal Dane. Oh, answer me! Let me not burst in ignorance; instead, tell me why your canonized bones — your bones that have been properly buried in a Christian graveyard and coffined in your death — have burst their funeral shroud. Tell me why the sepulcher, in which we saw you quietly buried, has opened its ponderous and marble jaws, and vomited you into the world of the living again. What is the meaning of this? Why are you, dead corpse, who is dressed again in a full suit of steel armor, revisiting the fitful gleams of flickering moonlight and making the night hideous? Why do you make we fools of nature so horridly tremble as we think about things that lie beyond the reaches of our souls? Why are you walking in the night? Why? What do you want us to do?"

The ghost motioned to Hamlet to follow him.

Horatio said, "It is beckoning you to follow and go away with it as if it had something important to tell you and you alone."

"Look," Marcellus said. "With a courteous motion, it waves at you to go to a more private place away from here. But do not go with it."

"No, by no means," Horatio said.

They were afraid for Hamlet. An evil spirit could tempt him to commit suicide.

"It will not speak to me here," Hamlet said, "and so I will follow it."

"Do not, my lord," Horatio said.

"Why, what should I be afraid of?" Hamlet asked. "I do not value my life as much as I do a pin. As for my soul, what can the ghost do to that — my soul is as immortal as the ghost is. It is again motioning to me to go with it. I will follow it."

"What if it tempts you toward the sea, my lord," Horatio asked, "or to the dreadful summit of the cliff that juts out over the sea? Suppose that it then assumes some other horrible form that might deprive you of your reason and make you insane? Think about this. Such a scene — you looking down many fathoms to the sea and hearing it roar — puts thoughts of desperation into every brain that sees and hears it."

"The ghost is still waving at me to follow it," Hamlet said.

He said to the ghost, "Lead on. I will follow you."

"You shall not go, my lord," Marcellus said.

Marcellus and Horatio physically restrained Hamlet, who told them, "Take away your hands."

"Listen to us," Horatio said. "You shall not follow the ghost."

"My fate cries out," Hamlet replied, "My destiny is calling to me. Every petty artery in my body is now as hardy as the Nemean lion's sinews. The Nemean lion was invulnerable, and so Hercules was unable to pierce its skin. He had to kill the lion by strangling it. The ghost still motions for me to come with it. Get your hands off me, gentlemen, or by Heaven, I'll make a ghost of whoever hinders me! I say, stay away from me!"

Marcellus and Horatio let go of Hamlet, who said to the ghost, "Go on; I'll follow you."

Hamlet and the ghost departed.

Horatio said, "Hamlet grows desperate and reckless with imagination and delusions."

"Let's follow him," Marcellus said. "We ought not to obey his orders to stay away from him. Obeying those orders would not be right."

"Yes, let's follow him," Horatio said. "What will be the result of this?"

"Something is rotten in the state of Denmark," Marcellus said.

"Heaven will take care of it," Horatio replied.

"Let's follow him," Marcellus said.

They went in the direction that Hamlet and the ghost had taken.

Hamlet stopped walking and asked the ghost, "Where are you leading me? I'll go no further."

"Listen to me carefully," the ghost said.

"I will."

"The hour has almost come when I must return to the sulfurous and tormenting flames of Purgatory."

"Alas, poor ghost!"

"Do not pity me," the ghost said. "Instead, listen carefully to what I shall tell you."

"Speak; I am bound by filial duty to hear you."

"When you hear what I have to say, you will be bound to seek revenge."

"What?"

"I am your father's spirit. I am doomed for a certain time to walk during the night, and during the day I am confined to fast in fires, until the foul sins I committed in my days of life are burnt and purged away. If I were not forbidden to tell the secrets of my prison-house, I could tell you things whose lightest word would harrow your soul, freeze your young blood, and make your two eyes, like falling stars, start from their sockets, and part your carefully arranged locks of hair and make each individual hair stand on end like the quills of the bad-tempered porcupine. But this revelation of the mysteries of Purgatory must not be made to ears of flesh and blood. Listen, listen, listen to me if you ever have loved your dear father —"

"Oh, God!"

"— revenge his foul and most unnatural murder."

"Murder!"

"Murder most foul," the ghost said. "Murder is foul at best, but my murder was very foul, strange, and unnatural. My murder is unnatural because it goes against the natural bonds of kinship."

"Quickly tell me what happened," Hamlet said, "so that I, with wings as swift as thinking or the thoughts of love, may sweep to my revenge."

"I find you apt and eager," the ghost said. "You would have to be duller than the overgrown weeds that root themselves in ease on the banks of the Lethe

River, whose water souls drink to forget past events, not to be moved by what I have to say.

"Now, Hamlet, listen. It was reported that as I was sleeping in my garden, a serpent bit me. The whole ear of Denmark is by a false account of my death rankly abused. Know, you noble youth, that the serpent that stung your father's life now wears his crown."

"Oh, my prophetic soul! I suspected this! My uncle!"

"Yes, your uncle is the cause of my death. He is an incestuous and adulterous beast. He used his knowledge of witchcraft, and he used traitorous gifts — wicked wit and gifts have the power to seduce! — to win to his shameful lust the will of my most seemingly virtuous Queen Gertrude, your mother.

"Oh, Hamlet, how she fell! She took her love from me, whose love was of such quality that it kept the vow I had made to her when I married her, and she gave it to a wretch whose natural gifts were poor in comparison to those of mine. True virtue can never be seduced even if lust dresses itself up with a Heavenly appearance, but lust, even if it has a Heavenly appearance, can first gorge itself in a celestial bed, and then gorge itself with garbage.

"But, wait! I think that I smell the morning air, so I must be brief. As I was sleeping — I thought safely — within my garden, as was my habit each afternoon, your uncle stole into my garden, carrying a vial of the poisonous juice of the cursed hebenon plant, and he poured the leprous poison into the shells of my ears. This poison so hates the blood of man that as quickly as it courses through the veins of the body, it makes the healthy and wholesome blood curdle like acid when dropped into milk. Quickly, my skin became like the bark of a tree. My skin became leprous; a vile and loathsome crust covered all my smooth body.

"That is how I, while sleeping, lost my life, my crown, and my queen, all because of a brother's hand. My life was cut short even in the blossom of my sin. I died without receiving the sacrament of holy communion, without confessing and being absolved from my sins, and without being anointed with holy oil. I was not given my last rites. I was not able to make a reckoning of my sins before I died, but instead I was sent to give an account of my sins with all my imperfections on my head. Oh, horrible! Oh, horrible! Most horrible!

"If you have any natural feeling in you, do not tolerate this. Do not allow the royal bed of Denmark to be a couch for lustfulness and damned incest. But, whatever you do, do not allow your mind to be corrupted by contact with your uncle, and do not plot to harm your mother. Leave her to Heaven and to her conscience — allow those thorns that lodge in her bosom to prick and sting her.

"Farewell now! The glowworm shows that the morning is near — the glowworm's ineffectual fire begins to pale.

"*Adieu, adieu*! Hamlet, remember me."

The ghost departed.

Hamlet said to himself, "Oh, all you host of Heaven — you angels! Oh, Earth! What else shall I call on? Shall I call on Hell? Damn! Do not break, my heart. And you, my sinews, do not grow instantly old, but instead keep me standing upright.

"Shall I remember you! Yes, you poor ghost, I will remember you for as long as memory holds a seat in this distracted globe — this head — of mine. Remember you! Yes, from the tablet of my memory I'll wipe away all trivial and foolish records, all quotations from books, all ideas, all past impressions and observations that I have copied and written there in my youth. The only thing that shall live on in the book and volume of my brain will be your commandment. It will not be mixed with baser matter. Yes, by Heaven!

"Oh, most pernicious woman! Oh, villain, villain, smiling, damned villain! My tablet — it is fitting that I write down that a person may smile, and smile, and still be a villain. At least I'm sure it may be so in Denmark."

Hamlet wrote on a tablet, and then he said, "So, uncle, there you are. Now to my watchword, aka motto — the words that I will live by. The ghost said, '*Adieu, adieu*! Remember me.' I have sworn to remember it."

Horatio called, "My lord! My lord!"

Marcellus called, "Lord Hamlet!"

"May Heaven protect Hamlet!" Horatio said.

Hamlet said to himself, "So be it."

Horatio called, "Hillo, ho, ho, my lord!"

A falconer uses the words "Hillo, ho, ho" to call his falcon to return to him.

Hamlet called back, "Hillo, ho, ho, boy! Come, bird, come."

Horatio and Marcellus walked over to Hamlet.

"How are you, my noble lord?" Marcellus asked.

"What happened, my lord?" Horatio asked.

"Something to be wondered at," Hamlet replied.

"My good lord, tell us what happened," Horatio requested.

"No; you'll reveal it."

"Not I, my lord," Horatio said. "I swear it by Heaven."

"I also swear that I will not reveal it," Marcellus said.

"What do you say then to this?" Hamlet said. "Would anyone ever think —"

He stopped and then asked, "But you will keep this secret?"

Horatio and Marcellus replied, "Yes, we will. We swear it by Heaven, my lord."

Hamlet thought about revealing to them what the ghost had said, but in the midst of speaking he changed his mind and said something obvious: "All complete and total villains dwelling in Denmark are ... complete and total knaves."

"No ghost, my lord, needs to come from the grave to tell us this," Horatio said. "We already know it."

"Why, you are right," Hamlet said. "You are in the right, and so, without any more explanation at all, I think it fitting that we shake hands and part. You shall do as your business and desire shall point you; every man has business and desire, such as it is. As for me, I will go and pray."

"These are wild and excited words, my lord," Horatio said.

"I'm sorry that they offend you," Hamlet said. "I am heartily sorry — yes, heartily."

"I am not offended," Horatio replied.

"By Saint Patrick you say that you are not offended," Hamlet said, "but my words are about offense — and a lot of offense. Regarding this vision here, it is an honest and genuine ghost — I can tell you that. As for your desire to know what happened between the ghost and me, stifle that desire as much as you are able to. And now, good friends, as you are friends, scholars, and soldiers, grant me one poor thing I request."

"What is it, my lord?" Horatio said. "We will grant it."

"Never make known what you have seen tonight," Hamlet said.

"My lord, we will not," both Horatio and Marcellus said.

"Swear it," Hamlet said.

"Truly, my lord, I will not reveal what I have seen tonight," Horatio said.

"Neither will I, truly," Marcellus said.

"Swear it upon the cross made by the hilt of my sword," Hamlet said.

Hamlet drew his sword.

"We have sworn, my lord, already," Marcellus said.

"Swear upon the cross made by the hilt of my sword," Hamlet repeated.

The ghost's voice came from under the ground: "Swear!"

"Ah, ha, boy!" Hamlet said, excitedly. "Do you say so? Are you there, truepenny — true and honest fellow?"

He said to Horatio and Marcellus, "Come on — you hear this fellow in the cellars — swear."

"Propose the oath you want us to swear to, my lord," Horatio said.

"Swear by my sword that you will never speak of this that you have seen."

The ghost's voice came from under the ground, but from a different spot than before: "Swear!"

Hamlet said about the ghost's voice, "*Hic et ubique*? [Latin for 'Here and everywhere?'] Then we'll shift our ground and move to a different spot. Come over here, gentlemen, and lay your hands again upon my sword. Swear by my sword that you will never tell what you have heard."

The ghost's voice came from under the ground, and again it came from a different spot than before: "Swear by his sword!"

"Well said, old mole!" Hamlet said. "Can you dig and work in the earth so fast? You are a worthy miner! Once more, let us move, good friends."

"Oh, day and night," Horatio said, "but this is wondrously strange!"

"Since the ghost is a stranger, welcome it," Hamlet said. "There are more things in Heaven and Earth, Horatio, than are dreamt of by philosophers."

He then said to both Horatio and Marcellus, "But come; swear here, as you have sworn oaths before, never, so help you God, no matter how strange or odd I act, as I perhaps hereafter shall think fitting to act in an antic and insane manner, that you, seeing me at such times, never shall do or say anything that reveals that you know that I am putting on an act. Swear that you will not fold your arms like this [Hamlet folded his arms], or shake your heads like this [Hamlet shook his head], or say some mysterious phrase such as 'Well, well, we know,' or 'We could, if we would,' or 'If we wanted to speak,' or 'There are people who could say more if they wanted to,' or such other ambiguous hint. In short, you will do nothing and you will say nothing that hints that you know that I am putting on an act. Swear this upon the grace and mercy that you will need on the Day of Judgment."

The ghost's voice came from under the ground: "Swear!"

Horatio and Marcellus put their hands on Hamlet's sword and swore not to tell what they had seen, not to tell what they had heard, and not to reveal that Hamlet was faking it when he acted as if he were insane.

"Rest, rest, perturbed spirit!" Hamlet said.

Hamlet then said to Horatio and Marcellus, "With all my love, I commend myself to you. Whatever so poor a man as Hamlet may do to express his love and friendship to you, God willing, he shall not stint to do. Let us go in together. Keep your fingers always on your lips, I ask you."

Hamlet made a 'shh!' sign with his finger on his lips, and then he added, "The time is disordered. Oh, cursed spirit, I regret that I was ever born to set it right!"

Horatio and Marcellus wanted Hamlet to enter the castle first, but Hamlet said to them, "No, let's go in together."

CHAPTER 2
— 2.1 —

In a room of his house, old Polonius was talking to Reynaldo, who was one of his servants. Laertes was now living in Paris, and Polonius was sending Reynaldo to him.

"Give him this money and these letters, Reynaldo," Polonius said.

"I will, my lord."

"You shall do a marvelous and wise thing, good Reynaldo, if, before you visit him, you inquire about his behavior in Paris."

"My lord, I intend to do that."

"Well said; very well said," Polonius said. "Look, sir, first inquire for me and find out which Danes are in Paris. Find out how they came to be there, who they are, how much money they have, and where they are living, what company they keep, and what are their expenses. If you find out that they know my son, you will learn more about him by using roundabout and vague questioning than if you were to question them directly about him. Pretend that you do not know him well, but that you have heard of him. You can say, 'I know his father and his friends, and I know him a little.' Do you understand me, Reynaldo?"

"Yes, very well, my lord."

"'— and I know him a little, but —' you may say '— not well, but if this person is the man I mean, he's very wild. He is addicted to so and so.' You can then charge him with whatever false accusations you please, but be careful not to charge him with any rank and disgraceful accusations that would dishonor him. Be careful not to do that. But, sir, you may charge him with such wanton, wild, and usual slips and faults that are commonly made by young men who are enjoying their first taste of liberty."

"Such as gambling, my lord?" Reynaldo asked.

"Yes, or drinking, fencing, swearing, quarrelling and fighting, visiting prostitutes — you may go so far as these things."

"My lord, that would dishonor him."

"In faith, no," Polonius said, "as long as you moderate the faults. You must not charge him with a major scandal, such as that he visits prostitutes every night — that is not what I want you to do. Instead, I want you to lightly talk about the slips and faults that come when a young man is first given his freedom — they are the flash and outbreak of a fiery mind, the wildness of an untamed young man, the things that happen to most young men."

"But, my good lord —"

"You want to know why I want you to do this?"

"Yes, my lord. I would like to know that."

"This is my scheme, and I believe that it is a legitimate scheme. You will charge my son in conversation with these slight sullies, as if they were like some spots of dirt that have soiled embroidery as it was being made. Young men often acquire slight sullies in the process of maturing. Listen to me. The person to whom you are talking, the person from whom you are seeking information about my son's conduct, if he has ever seen my son commit any of the sins that we have mentioned, he will confirm my son's fault, and he will call you 'good sir,' or something similar, or 'friend,' or 'gentleman,' according to the form of address used by his social class and his country."

"Very good, my lord."

"And then, sir, he will do this — he will do — what was I about to say? By the Mass, I was about to say something. Where did I leave off?"

"You said that the person I was speaking to would confirm your son's fault, if he is guilty, and would call me 'good sir,' or something similar, or 'friend,' or 'gentleman.'"

"Yes," Polonius said. "He will confirm my son's fault by saying something like this: 'I know the gentleman. I saw him yesterday, or the other day, or this day, or that day. And as you said, he was gambling, or drinking to excess, or playing court tennis.' Or perhaps he will say, 'I saw him enter such a house of sale.' *Videlicet* [Latin for 'That is to say'], a brothel. And so forth.

"Do you see? Your bait of falsehood will capture the prize of truth. We men of wisdom and of foresight use roundabout courses and devious tests to find out information and truth. If you follow this lecture and my advice, you shall learn the truth about my son. You understand me, don't you?"

"I do, my lord," Reynaldo replied.

"May God be with you," Polonius said. "Farewell."

"Goodbye, my lord."

"Use your eyes when you are with my son. Go along with whatever he wants to do."

"I shall, my lord."

"And let him ply his music, whatever his music might be."

"That is good advice, my lord."

"Farewell!"

Reynaldo left the room just as Ophelia, Polonius' daughter, entered it. Ophelia looked distressed.

"How are you, Ophelia! What's the matter?"

"Oh, my lord, my lord, I have been so frightened!"

"Frightened by what, in the name of God?"

"My lord, as I was sewing in my private chamber, Lord Hamlet — with his jacket all unbuttoned, no hat on his head, wearing dirty stockings without garters so that his stockings had fallen down and were like fetters around his ankles, pale as his shirt, his knees knocking each other, and with a look so piteous that it seemed as if he had been released from Hell so that he could speak of his horrors — came to me."

"Is he insane because he loves you?" Polonius asked.

"My father, I do not know," Ophelia replied, "but truly, I am afraid that that is true."

"What did he say?"

"He took me by the wrist and held me hard, and then he backed up until he was at his arm's length, and holding his other hand over his brow, he stared at my face as if he were going to draw it. He stayed like that a long time, but at last, shaking my arm a little, and waving his head up and down three times, he sighed so piteously and profoundly that it seemed to shatter his entire body and end his life. Having finished that, he let me go, and turning his head over his shoulder, he left my private chamber without the use of his eyes. He went out of doors without looking where he was going — he kept staring at me as he left."

"Come with me," Polonius said. "I will go and seek the King. Hamlet is in the very ecstasy and madness of love, whose violent nature destroys itself and leads the will to desperate undertakings as often as any passion under Heaven that does afflict our natures. This madness has enough violence that it can cause self-destruction. I am sorry that Hamlet is insane. Have you spoken to him any hard words recently?"

"No, my good lord," Ophelia replied. "I have done only what you commanded me to do. I returned his letters, and I have declined to let him visit me."

"That has made him insane," Polonius said. "I am sorry that I have not observed him with better heed and judgment. I was afraid that he was trifling with you and that he wanted to ruin you. Curse my suspicious nature! By Heaven, old people are just as likely to be overly suspicious as young people are to be indiscreet.

"Come, let's go to the King. We must give him this information. He will not want to hear it, but it might cause more harm to keep it secret than to reveal it."

— 2.2 —

In a room in the castle, King Claudius, Queen Gertrude, Rosencrantz, and Guildenstern were speaking. Also present were various attendants.

"Welcome, dear Rosencrantz and Guildenstern!" King Claudius said. "We have much wanted to see you, but in addition, we need you to do something for us and so we sent a message to you to come quickly to us. You must have heard something about a change in Hamlet. We can say that he has been transformed since he is different both outside and inside. Neither the exterior nor the inward man resembles what it was.

"What the cause of this transformation, other than his father's death, can be, I cannot dream. Therefore, I ask you both, since from childhood you have been brought up with him, and since you know his youth and behavior so well, to agree to stay here in our court for a little while. That way, you two can encourage Hamlet to engage in pleasurable activities, and we hope that you can learn whether there is something, unknown to us, that is afflicting him — something that, once we know what it is, we can set to rights."

"Good gentlemen," Queen Gertrude said, "Hamlet has talked a lot about you, and I am sure that there are not two men living with whom he is friendlier. If it will please you to show us so much gentlemanly courtesy and good will as to spend time with us for a while, and to help us, we will reward your visit with such thanks as only a King can give."

Rosencrantz replied, "Both your majesties can, by the sovereign power you have over us, simply command rather than request us to do something."

"But we will both obey you," Guildenstern said, "and here we give up ourselves, and we fully and freely lay our service at your feet. Command us as you will."

"Thanks, Rosencrantz and gentle Guildenstern," King Claudius said.

"Thanks, Guildenstern and gentle Rosencrantz," Queen Gertrude said, adding, "I ask you to immediately visit my too-much-changed son."

She said to the attendants, "Go, some of you. Take these gentlemen to where Hamlet is."

"May the Heavens make our presence and our actions pleasant and helpful to him!" Guildenstern replied.

"Amen!" Queen Gertrude said.

Rosencrantz, Guildenstern, and some attendants departed.

Polonius entered the room and said, "The ambassadors from Norway, my good lord, have returned. They are joyful."

"You have always been the father of good news," King Claudius said.

"Have I, my lord?" Polonius replied. "I assure my good liege that I perform my duty to both my God and my King as carefully as I guard my soul."

He added, "I think, or else this brain of mine is not as able as it used to be to follow a track or scent that requires a knowledge of men and political affairs, that I have found the cause of Hamlet's lunacy."

"Tell us the cause," King Claudius said. "I very much want to know that."

"First allow the ambassadors to come here and give you their news," Polonius said. "My news shall be the fruit — the dessert — to that great feast."

"You may do the honors of welcoming the ambassadors and bringing them in here," King Claudius replied.

Polonius left to do his duty.

King Claudius said to Queen Gertrude, "He tells me, my dear Gertrude, that he has found the head and source — the cause — of your son's illness."

"I doubt that it is anything but what we most suspect it is: his father's death and our very quick marriage."

"Well, we shall question Polonius thoroughly."

Polonius returned, bringing with him King Claudius' ambassadors to Norway: Voltemand and Cornelius.

King Claudius said, "Welcome, my good friends! Tell me, Voltemand, what news do you bring us from our fellow ruler the King of Norway?"

"I bring very fair greetings from him to you, and I bring a very fair answer to your requests of him. Immediately after our first meeting with him, he sent out men to stop his nephew from drafting men into an army. The King of Norway had thought that his nephew was raising an army to attack Poland, but after an investigation, he found that the army was actually being raised to attack your highness. Once he learned that, he was aggrieved and angry that he had been deceived in his sickness, old age, and lack of strength. He sent orders to young Fortinbras to stop preparing for war and to appear before him. Fortinbras came to the castle, received a rebuke from the King of Norway, and in the end vowed to his uncle the King that he would never again plan to make war against your majesty. Hearing this, the old King of Norway, overcome with joy, gave him an annuity of three thousand crowns, and he gave him permission to use his soldiers to make war against Poland. With that in mind, he gave us a document that entreats you for permission for Fortinbras' army to cross Denmark so the soldiers can make war against Poland."

Voltemand handed King Claudius a document and said, "The King of Norway hopes that you will give your permission to this enterprise. This document lays down guarantees for the safety of Denmark if you allow the Norwegian army to cross it."

"We like this well," King Claudius said, using the royal plural. He added, "And when we have more time to consider this matter, we will read this document carefully, send an answer to the King of Norway, and think about the far-reaching consequences that can follow what we decide.

"In the meantime, we thank you for your successfully undertaken labor. Go and rest now; at night we'll feast together. Most welcome home!"

Voltemand and Cornelius departed.

Polonius said, "This business is well ended. My liege, and madam, to make a speech about what a King should be, what duty is, why day is day, night is night, and time is time, would accomplish nothing but to waste night, day, and time. Therefore, since brevity is the soul of wit, and tediousness is the limbs and outward flourishes, I will be brief. Your noble son is mad; he is insane. Mad call I it; because, to define true madness, what is true madness except to be nothing else but mad? But let that go."

Queen Gertrude said, "More matter, with less art. More content, with fewer rhetorical flourishes."

Polonius replied, "Madam, I swear I use no rhetorical flourishes at all. That Hamlet is mad, it is true. It is true that his madness is a pity, and it is a pity that it is true. But these are rhetorical flourishes, so I will stop using them, because I do not want to use rhetorical flourishes.

"Let us grant that Hamlet is mad, then. What now remains is to discover the cause of this effect, or I should better say, to discover the cause of this defect, because this defective effect has a cause. Thus it remains, and that is the remainder. Perpend. Listen carefully. I have a daughter — I have her while she is mine, which is until she marries — who, in her duty and obedience to me, you see, has given me this. Now gather, and think about this."

He began to read a letter — written by Hamlet to Ophelia — out loud:

"*To the celestial, and my soul's idol, the most beautified Ophelia,*

"That's an ill word, a vile word; 'beautified' is a vile word: but you shall hear the rest of the letter. Here it is:

"*In her excellent white bosom, this letter, & etc.*"

Queen Gertrude asked, "Did Hamlet write this letter to her?"

"Good madam, wait awhile," Polonius said. "As I said that I would do, I will read the rest of the letter:

"*Doubt that the stars are fire;*

"*Doubt that the Sun does move;*

"*Suspect truth to be a liar;*

"*But never doubt I love.*

"*Oh, dear Ophelia, I am bad at writing poetry like this. I do not have the art to count my groans — or to make them scan as poetry. However, believe that I love you best — oh, most best — believe it.* Adieu.

"*Yours evermore, most dear lady, while this complex body belongs to him,* HAMLET.

"This letter, in obedience to me, my daughter has shown me. Hamlet also wrote other letters to her. My daughter has told me about his courting of her and at what times and places these acts of courtship occurred."

"How has she reacted to his courtship of her?" King Claudius asked.

"What do you think about me?"

"I think that you are a faithful and honorable man," King Claudius said.

"I hope to prove to be that," Polonius replied. "But what would you have thought if, after I had seen this hot love on the wing — and I perceived it, I must tell you, before my daughter told me — what would you, or my dear majesty your Queen here, have thought if I had been like a notebook and simply recorded the information in my brain and kept silent about it? What if I had closed my eyes to it and kept mute and dumb, or if I had looked upon this love and done nothing? What would you have thought? No, I did not keep quiet. Instead, I took action and I said to my daughter, 'Lord Hamlet is a Prince, and he is out of your league. This must not be.' I then gave her orders to lock herself away from his presence, to admit no messengers from him, to receive no tokens of love. She did all these things. Hamlet, repelled by her — a short tale to say — fell into a sadness and depression, then into a fast because of loss of appetite, from thence into insomnia, from thence into a debility, from thence into a delirium, and, by this decline after decline, he finally fell into the madness wherein now he raves, and all of us mourn for him."

King Claudius asked Queen Gertrude, "Do you think that this is true?"

"It very likely is."

"Has there ever been a time — I'd like to know — that I have positively said, 'It is so,' and it turned out not to be so?" Polonius asked.

"Not that I know of," King Claudius replied.

Polonius said, "Take my staff of office from my hand, if what I have said turns out not to be true. If I have relevant evidence, I will follow it and will find where the truth is hidden even if it were hidden in the center of the Earth."

"How may we test whether this is true?" King Claudius asked.

"You know that sometimes Hamlet walks for four or so hours together here in the lobby," Polonius said.

"So he does indeed," Queen Gertrude said.

"At one of those times, I'll loose my daughter so she can go to him."

Polonius was unaware of the implications of the word "loose." On a farm, an animal can be loosed so that it will have sex.

He continued, "King Claudius, you and I will be hidden behind an arras — a wall hanging — and we will witness their encounter. If we find out that Hamlet does not love my daughter and that his love for her is not the reason why he is mad, then let me be no longer a minister of state in your court; instead, I will take care of a farm and wagons."

"We will try your plan," King Claudius said.

"Look," Queen Gertrude said. "Hamlet, the poor wretch, is coming here while reading."

"Leave now," Polonius said to King Claudius and Queen Gertrude. "Please leave now. I will talk to him alone. Please allow me to do that."

King Claudius, Queen Gertrude, and the remaining servants left the room, leaving behind Polonius and Hamlet.

Polonius asked, "How is my good Lord Hamlet?"

"I am well. May God have mercy on you."

"Do you know who I am, my lord?"

"I know you very well," Hamlet replied. "You are a fishmonger — a seller of fish."

"I am not, my lord," Polonius said.

"In that case, I wish that you were as honest as a fishmonger."

"Honest, my lord?"

"Yes, sir," Hamlet said. "To be an honest man, as this world goes, is to be one man picked out of ten thousand."

"That's very true, my lord."

Hamlet read out loud from his book, "*For if the Sun breed maggots in a dead dog, being a good kissing carrion —*"

People in Hamlet's time and society believed that the Sun shining on — kissing — a corpse causes maggots to come into existence — they did not realize that flies laid eggs on the corpse and maggots hatched out of those eggs.

Hamlet then asked, "Do you have a daughter?"

"I have, my lord."

"Do not allow her to walk in the Sun. Conception is a blessing, but it would not be a blessing if your daughter were to conceive. Friend, be careful concerning your daughter."

Hamlet was punning — and speaking inappropriately — about Polonius' daughter: Ophelia. "Walk in the Sun" can mean "walk in public" or "be made pregnant by the Sun" — if the Sun can bring to life maggots, why can't it bring to life a human infant? "Conception" can mean "(the ability) to form ideas" or "(the ability) to become pregnant." "Conceive" can mean "form ideas" or "become pregnant." Also, Hamlet transitioned from saying the term "kissing carrion" to talking about Ophelia. "Carrion" is a contemptuous term for flesh available for sexual pleasure.

Polonius thought, *How about that! He is still thinking and talking about my daughter. But he did not recognize me at first; he said that I was a fishmonger. He is far gone, far gone in his madness. Truly in my youth I suffered very deep distress because I was in love; my distress was very close to this distress that Hamlet is feeling. I'll speak to him again.*

Polonius asked, "What are you reading, my lord?"

"Words, words, words."

"What is the matter, my lord?"

"Between whom?"

"I mean the subject matter that you are reading, my lord."

Hamlet replied, "I am reading about slanders, sir. The satirical rogue — the author — says here that old men have grey beards, that their faces are wrinkled, their eyes discharge thick amber sap and plum-tree gum, and they have a plentiful lack of wit, together with very weak legs. Although I most powerfully and potently believe all of these things, sir, yet I do not think that it is courteous to have it thus written down. You yourself, sir, should be as old as I am, if like a crab you could go backward."

Polonius thought, *Though these words are mad, yet there is some sort of meaning in them. Hamlet is ill; he should not be in this cold air.*

Polonius asked, "Will you walk out of this air, my lord?"

"Into my grave," Hamlet replied.

"Indeed, your grave is out of this air," Polonius said.

He thought, *How pregnant with meaning his replies sometimes are! Madness often hits on a happiness of meaning, although reason and sanity could not so quickly and happily come up with that meaning. I will leave Hamlet, and I will quickly contrive a meeting between my daughter and him.*

He said to Hamlet, "My honorable lord, I will most humbly take my leave of you. Goodbye."

"You cannot, sir, take from me anything that I will more willingly part with — except my life, except my life, except my life."

"Fare you well, my lord."

Hamlet said as Polonius walked away, "These tedious old fools!"

Rosencrantz and Guildenstern entered the room.

Polonius said to them, "You must be seeking the Lord Hamlet; there he is."

Rosencrantz replied, "May God save you, sir!"

Polonius departed.

Guildenstern said to Hamlet, "My honored lord!"

Rosencrantz said to Hamlet, "My most dear lord!"

Hamlet replied, "My excellent good friends! How are you, Guildenstern? Ah, Rosencrantz! Good lads, how are you two?"

Rosencrantz replied, "We are ordinary children of the Earth."

"We are happy in that we are not too happy," Guildenstern said. "We are not on the button at the very top of Fortune's cap. We are not riding high on Fortune's wheel."

"Are you down so low that you sit at the soles of her shoes?" Hamlet asked.

"We live neither high nor low, my lord," Rosencrantz said.

"Then do you live about her waist, or in the middle of her favors?" Hamlet asked.

"Indeed, we are the privates of her army. We are ordinary."

"If you are her privates, you must live in the vicinity of her private and secret parts. This is not a surprise. Lady Fortune is a strumpet," Hamlet said.

Many people regarded Lady Fortune as being a strumpet — a whore or promiscuous woman. She both gave and withheld good things indiscriminately. She was a fickle goddess — she was faithful to no man.

Hamlet asked them, "What's the news?"

"There is no news, my lord, except that the world's grown honest," Rosencrantz said.

"Then Doomsday — the Day of Judgment — must be near," Hamlet said. "That is the only thing that could make all the people of the world turn honest. But your news is not true. Let me make my question more specific: What have you, my good friends, done to be sent by Lady Fortune to this prison here?"

"Prison, my lord!" Guildenstern said.

"Denmark's a prison," Hamlet said.

"In that case, the world is a prison," Rosencrantz said.

"The world is a spacious and fine prison," Hamlet said. "In this world are many places of confinement, prison wards, and dungeons — and Denmark is one of the worst."

"We think that that is not so, my lord," Rosencrantz said.

"Why, then, it is not a prison to you," Hamlet said, "because there is nothing either good or bad, except that thinking makes it so. To me, Denmark is a prison."

Hamlet thought, *There is nothing either good or bad, except that thinking makes it so. How much truth, if any, does that statement have? One's attitude can affect how we regard something. If I feel that Denmark is a prison to me, then it is a prison to me. But is it true that no objective right and no objective wrong exist?*

"Why, then your ambition makes Denmark a prison; it is too narrow for your mind," Rosencrantz said.

"Oh, God, I could be confined in a nutshell and consider myself a King of infinite space, were it not that I have bad dreams," Hamlet replied.

"Such dreams indeed are ambition, for the very substance of the ambitious is merely the shadow of a dream," Guildenstern said.

"A dream itself is but a shadow," Hamlet replied.

"Truly, and I think that ambition is of so airy and light a quality that it is but a shadow's shadow," Rosencrantz said.

"If that is correct, then only beggars have solid bodies because beggars have no ambition," Hamlet said. "Our Kings and heroes are then the shadows of the beggars because Kings and heroes are ambitious and therefore shadows, and they must be the shadows of something. The shadows of the heroes are stretched out like shadows early in the morning or late in the afternoon. But perhaps we should go inside the court because my reasoning powers are going wacky."

"We'll attend you and be your servants," Rosencrantz and Guildenstern said.

"No," Hamlet said. "I will not class you with the rest of my servants because, to tell you honestly, I am most dreadfully attended to. But, in the direct way that friends talk to one another, let me ask you this: Why are you here at Elsinore?"

"To visit you, my lord," Rosencrantz said. "No other reason."

"I am poor even in thanks, but I thank you," Hamlet said. "But surely, dear friends, my thanks are too dear a halfpenny."

Did Hamlet mean that his thanks were not worth a halfpenny because he lacked power in Denmark — his uncle, not Hamlet, had become King after Hamlet's father died? Or did Hamlet mean that Rosencrantz and Guildenstern did not deserve even his poor thanks, which were worth only a halfpenny? If so, Hamlet was already suspecting that King Claudius was using Rosencrantz and Guildenstern to spy on him. If Rosencrantz and Guildenstern were spying on Hamlet, then the two men deserved no thanks from Hamlet.

Hamlet then asked, "Weren't you sent for and asked to come to the court? Did you come here of your own free will? Did you come here voluntarily or were you asked to come here? Come, deal justly with me. Come, come; speak up."

Guildenstern asked, "What should we say, my lord?"

Hamlet replied, "Why, anything except something that is to the purpose."

Hamlet did not expect a straight answer — a true answer — from Rosencrantz and Guildenstern.

He then said, "You were sent for; and there is a kind of confession in your looks that your modesties have not craft enough to color. You cannot hide the truth. I know the good King and Queen have sent for you."

"For what purpose, my lord?" Rosencrantz asked.

"That you must teach me," Hamlet replied. "But let me ask you solemnly, by the rights of our fellowship, by the harmonious friendship of our youth, by the obligation of our ever-preserved friendship, and by whatever is more dear that a better proposer than I could mention to you, be even and direct with me. Answer me truthfully: Did someone send for you, or not?"

Rosencrantz whispered to Guildenstern, "What do you think we should say?"

Hamlet thought, *I will keep my eyes on you two.*

He said out loud, "If you regard me as a friend, answer me truthfully."

"My lord, we were sent for," Guildenstern said.

"I will tell you why," Hamlet said. "No doubt you have promised not to speak honestly to me, and if I tell you why you were sent for, then you do not have to tell me why, and so you can keep your promise to the King and Queen.

"I have recently — but I do not know why — lost all my mirth, neglected my usual occupations; and indeed my mood is so depressed that this good structure, the Earth, seems to me a sterile promontory. I am so depressed that this very excellent canopy, the air — listen to me — this splendid overhanging firmament, this majestic roof decorated with the golden fire we call the Sun — why, it appears as no other thing to me than a foul and pestilent congregation of vapors.

"What a piece of work is a man! How noble in reason! How infinite in faculty! In form and movement, how expressive and admirable! In action, how like an angel! In apprehension and understanding, how like a god! Man is the beauty of the world! Man is the paragon — the pattern of excellence — of animals! And yet, to me, what is this quintessence of dust?"

Hamlet thought, *Genesis 3:19 states, "In the sweat of thy face shalt thou eat bread till thou return to the earth: for out of it wast thou taken, because thou art dust, and to dust shalt thou return."*

He continued, "Man does not delight me — no — nor does woman, although by your smiling I judge that you seem to think so."

"My lord, there was no such stuff in my thoughts," Rosencrantz said.

"Why did you laugh, then, when I said, 'Man does not delight me'?"

"I was thinking, my lord, that if you do not delight in man, then some actors who are coming here will receive a Lenten entertainment from you," Rosencrantz replied. "Lent is a time of fasting and a time when the theaters are closed, and so a Lenten entertainment is a poor entertainment. On our way here, we passed a troupe of actors who are coming here to offer you their service."

"He who plays the King shall be welcome; his majesty shall receive tribute from me," Hamlet said. "The adventurous knight shall use his rapier and small shield. The lover shall not sigh for free but shall be paid. The eccentric man shall perform his part and end it in peace. The clown shall make laugh audience members who laugh easily when their lungs are tickled. The boy actor playing the lady shall speak the part freely and well, or else the blank verse of the part shall limp because it is badly spoken.

"Which actors are they?"

"You have seen them before," Rosencrantz replied. "You used to enjoy seeing them — they are the tragedians of the city."

"Why are they traveling on tour?" Hamlet asked. "Their performing in their home city is better both for their reputation and for their profit."

"I think that they have been banned from performing in their home city because of some recent political unrest and disturbances."

"Do they have the same reputation that they had when I was in the city?" Hamlet asked. "Are they as popular now as they were then?"

"No, indeed, they are not," Rosencrantz said.

"Why not? Have they grown rusty?"

"No, they are as good as they have ever been, but there is, sir, a nest of children, little baby hawks, who squawk louder than anyone else, and who are most excessively applauded for it. These child actors are now the fashion, and they so abuse the common stages — so people call the public theaters — that many fashionable gentlemen wearing rapiers scarcely dare to attend the theaters featuring adult actors because of the goose-quills wielded by poets writing plays for the child actors. In short, the fashionable gentlemen are afraid to attend the theaters featuring adult actors because the poets writing plays for the child actors will satirize them."

"What? These rival actors are children?" Hamlet asked. "Who takes care of them? How are they maintained financially? Will they pursue the profession of acting no longer than they can sing? Will they stop acting once their voice breaks? Will they not say afterwards, if they should grow up and become adult actors — as is very likely, if their means of financial support are no better than they are now — their writers do them wrong, to make them exclaim against their own future profession?"

"Truly, both sides have been doing a lot of arguing," Rosencrantz said, "and the nation holds it to be no sin to incite them to quarrel. There was, for a while, no money bid for a new play unless the plot led to a fight between the adult actors and the playwrights who write for the child actors."

"Is this possible?" Hamlet asked.

"Oh, there has been much throwing about of brains," Guildenstern said. "Much mental activity has been expended in this quarrel."

"Do the child actors triumph?"

"Yes, they do, my lord," Rosencrantz said. "They carry the victor's crown the way that Hercules once carried the entire world when he took the burden off Atlas."

"This change in popularity is not very strange," Hamlet said. "My uncle is now King of Denmark, and those people who would make faces at him while my father still lived and ruled as King, now give twenty, forty, fifty, or a hundred ducats apiece for miniatures of his portrait.

"Such things commonly happen, but why? By God's blood, there is something in this that is more than natural, if philosophy could find it out. Scientific inquiry may be able to find the cause."

Trumpets sounded. The troupe of actors blew trumpets in towns and before castles to advertise their presence.

Guildenstern said, "There are the actors."

Hamlet said to Rosencrantz and Guildenstern, "Gentlemen, you are welcome to Elsinore. Let us shake hands. Come on. The proper accompaniment of welcome is fashion and ceremony. Let me comply with all of that by shaking your hands. I will greet the actors with a friendly welcome, and I do not want you to think that I welcome them more than I welcome you. You are welcome, but my uncle-father and aunt-mother are deceived."

"In what, my dear lord?" Guildenstern asked.

"I am not insane all the time," Hamlet said. "I am only mad when the wind is blowing from the north-north-west. When the wind is blowing from the south, I know a hawk from a handsaw."

Such words could only make Rosencrantz and Guildenstern suspect that Hamlet was mad, or on the verge of madness, all the time, but Hamlet may have given the two men a hidden warning. He knew the difference between two dissimilar things such as a hawk and a handsaw, and so he also knew the difference between two dissimilar things such as an enemy and a friend.

Polonius walked over to the three men.

"May you gentlemen be well," Polonius said.

"Listen, Guildenstern — and you, too, Rosencrantz," Hamlet said. "I want a hearer at each of my ears. That great big baby you see there is not yet out of his swaddling clothes."

"Perhaps this is the second time of his life that he has to wear them," Rosencrantz said, "because they say that an old man becomes a child for the second time."

"I will prophesy that he has come here to tell me of the arrival of the actors," Hamlet said. "Wait and see."

He then pretended to be in the middle of a conversation: "You are correct, sir. On Monday morning — that was the time indeed."

"My lord, I have news to tell you," Polonius said to Hamlet.

"My lord, I have news to tell you," Hamlet replied. "When Roscius was an actor in Rome —"

The famous Roman actor Roscius died in 62 B.C.E.

"A troupe of actors have come here, my lord," Polonius said.

"Buzz, buzz! Yawn! This is old news!" Hamlet said.

"On my honor —" Polonius began to say.

"— then came each actor on his ass," Hamlet said.

"— they are the best actors in the world," Polonius said, "whether for tragedy, comedy, history, pastoral plays, pastoral-comical plays, historical-pastoral plays, tragical-historical plays, tragical-comical-historical-pastoral plays, plays that observe the unities of action and time and place, or plays that do not. Seneca's tragedies are not too heavy and serious for them, and Plautus' comedies are not too light for them. For the law of writ and for the liberty, these are the only men — these actors perform well whether they are strictly following prescribed rules or performing more freely and loosely."

"Oh, Jephthah, judge of Israel, what a treasure you had!" Hamlet said.

"What a treasure he had, my lord?" Polonius asked.

"Why," Hamlet said, and then he sang these lines:

"*One fair daughter he had and no more,*

"*Whom he loved surpassingly well.*"

Polonius thought, *He is still thinking about my daughter.*

"Am I not right, old Jephthah?" Hamlet asked Polonius.

Jephthah was a King of Israel who made a rash vow. When he went off to fight the Ammonites, he vowed to God that if he were victorious that he would then sacrifice to God the first thing that he saw coming out of the door of his house when he returned from battle. The first thing that he saw coming of the door of his house was his daughter, and he sacrificed her.

"If you call me Jephthah, my lord," Polonius said, "I have a daughter whom I love surpassingly well."

"No, that does not follow," Hamlet said.

One can wonder whether Jephthah should have kept his vow and just how much he loved his daughter.

"What follows, then, my lord?"

"Why," Hamlet said, and then he sang this line:

"*As by lot God wot [knows].*"

Hamlet added, "And then, you know," and he sang this line:

"*It came to pass most like it was —*"

He added, "The first row of the pious chanson will show you more."

This is the beginning of the pious chanson, aka religious ballad:

I read that many years ago,

When Jepha Judge of Israel.

Had one fair daughter and no more,

Whom he loved so passing [surpassingly] well.

And as by lot God wot

It came to pass most like it was

Great wars there should be,

And who should be the chief, but he, but he.

The ballad then told the rest of the story. In the story were many rows, aka conflicts. The first conflict was that between nations: Israel versus Ammon. Other conflicts were between duty to God and duty to kin — in this case, a daughter.

In Dante's *Paradise*, Dante the Pilgrim travels throughout the universe until he reaches the Mystic Empyrean, the dwelling place of God. On the Moon, he speaks to Piccarda Donati, who tells him that Jephthah's vow was blind and rash, and he did evil by keeping it. Far better would have been for him to say, "My vow was wrong," and not keep it. Such a vow as Jephthah's is not the kind that God approves. Piccarda's main advice to Dante, and to Christians, is to not make rash vows.

Like Jephthah, Hamlet must decide where his duty lies. What is his duty to his father? What is his duty to God? Do these duties conflict? If they conflict, what ought he to do?

When Hamlet said, "The first row of the pious chanson will show you more," the word "row" could mean "line" or even "stanza." Reading the first line or stanza of the religious ballad will provide more information, but it will not tell the entire story. Of course, "row" can also mean "quarrel" or "conflict."

We can predict the consequences of our actions, but often we do not know what the consequences — even the serious consequences — will be. Jephthah probably thought that a dog, not his daughter, would be the first thing he saw coming out of the door of his house after he returned from war. Often, we do not know the consequences of our actions until we do the actions. Hamlet must choose to act — or choose not to act — with incomplete information.

Hamlet added, "Look, my abridgement is coming."

Hamlet's conversation was being shortened by the arrival of the actors, who also abridge, or shorten, time by putting on entertaining plays that make time pass quickly.

The actors walked up to the group of men.

"You are welcome, masters; welcome, all," Hamlet greeted them. He recognized each of them. "I am glad to see that you are well. Welcome, good friends. Oh, my old friend! your face is valenced — fringed — with a beard since I saw you last. Have you come here to beard me in Denmark?"

This was a joke. To beard someone was a major insult — someone would pull out a few hairs from the beard of someone and throw them in his face.

Hamlet said to a boy who played female characters, "What, my young lady and mistress! By Our Lady the Virgin Mary, your ladyship is nearer to Heaven than when I saw you last, by the altitude of a heel on a shoe. You have grown taller. Pray to God that your voice, like a piece of uncurrent gold, be not cracked within the ring."

This was another joke by Hamlet. Gold coins of the time bore the face of a King enclosed in a circle. Dishonest people would sometimes trim gold from the edges of coins. If they trimmed too much gold off the edge, so that the trimming — or crack — went inside the circle, then the coin became uncurrent — no longer legal tender. When the boy reached puberty and his voice began to crack, he would no longer be able to play the parts of female characters.

Hamlet's joke included a bawdy aspect. The ring is an O, which is a symbol for a vagina. If the O is cracked, aka entered, the woman loses her virginity.

Hamlet continued, "Masters, you are all welcome. We'll even have a go at it — the recitation of a speech — like French falconers, whose falcons fly at anything, including the first thing they see. We won't wait; instead, we'll have the recitation of a speech right now. Come, give us a taste of the quality of your acting; come, give us a passionate speech."

The first actor asked, "What speech do you want to hear, my lord?"

"I heard you recite a speech once," Hamlet replied, "but it was never acted; or, if it was, it was acted only once because the play, I remember, pleased not the millions. It was like caviar to the general public — too refined a taste for them to be able to enjoy. But it was — as I regarded it, and others, whose judgments in such matters are better than mine — an excellent play, well organized in the scenes, set down with as much modest restraint as cunning skill. I remember that one critic said that there were no sharp flavors, aka bawdy bits, in the lines to make them spicy, and there was nothing in the lines that might make the author guilty of affectation. The critic called the play unpretentious, as wholesome as sweet, and with much more natural grace than affectation and showiness.

"One speech in it I chiefly loved: It was Aeneas' tale to Dido. I especially liked the part where he speaks about the slaughter of Priam."

Hamlet was referring to the end of the Trojan War, which had started when Paris, a Prince from Troy, had run away with Helen, the wife of King Menelaus of Sparta in Greece. For ten years a Greek army besieged Troy but was unable to conquer it. Finally, Odysseus came up with the idea of the Trojan Horse. A Greek named Epeus built a huge, hollow horse that the Trojans thought was an offering to the goddess Athena. Inside the hollow horse Greek soldiers hid. The Trojans pulled the Trojan Horse inside the city, and at night the Greek soldiers came out of the horse and went to the city gates and let in the rest of the Greek army, which had pretended to sail back to Greece. One of the Greeks inside the Trojan Horse was Pyrrhus, the son of Achilles. After Achilles died at Troy, Pyrrhus went to fight in the Trojan War to avenge the death of his father. During the fall of Troy, its King, Priam, wore ancient armor and carried a weapon although he was much too old to fight. Pyrrhus found and killed the aged King Priam, whose son Paris had run away with Helen and started the war.

Hamlet said, "If you remember the speech, begin at this line — let me see, let me see,

"The rugged Pyrrhus, like the Hyrcanian beast —"

Hyrcania was famous for its ferocious tigers.

Hamlet said, "Wait, that's not right, but it does begin with 'Pyrrhus' —

"The rugged and terrifying Pyrrhus, he whose sable armor,

"Black as his purpose, resembled the night

"When he lay hidden in the ominous horse,

"Has now this dread and black complexion smeared

"With a color more calamitous; from head to foot

"Now is he totally red; he is horridly covered

"With the blood of Trojan fathers, mothers, daughters, sons,

"Baked and crusted from the fires in Trojan streets,

"Fires that lend a tyrannous and damned light

"To their King's murder. Roasted in wrath and fire,

"And glazed with coagulated gore,

"With eyes like carbuncles that glow in the dark, the Hellish Pyrrhus

"Old grandfather Priam seeks."

Hamlet said to the first actor, "Continue from where I left off."

Polonius said to Hamlet, "Before God, my lord, I say that your recitation was well spoken, with both good delivery and good taste."

The first player recited this speech:

"Quickly Pyrrhus finds Priam

"Striking at Greeks with blows that fall short; his antique sword,

"Which will not obey his arm, lies where it falls,

"Refusing to obey his will. Unequally matched,

"Pyrrhus at Priam drives; in rage he strikes and misses;

"But with the whiff and wind of his deadly sword

"The enfeebled father Priam falls. Then the senseless citadel of Ilium — Troy

—

"Seeming to feel this blow, with flaming top

"Falls to its base, and with a hideous crash

"Deafens the ears of Pyrrhus. Look! His sword,

"Which was falling on the milky-white head

"Of revered Priam, seemed in the air to stick.

"So, like a painted portrait of a tyrant, motionless, Pyrrhus stood,

"And as if he had lost interest in what he was doing,

"Did nothing.

"But, as we often see, predicting some storm,

"A silence in the Heavens, the high clouds stand still,

"The bold winds are without speech and the orb below is

"As quiet as death, as soon as the dreadful thunder

"Rends the air, likewise, after Pyrrhus' pause,

"Aroused vengeance sets him back to work.

"Never did the Cyclopes' hammers fall as they created

"The armor of Mars, god of war, that they forged for eternal strength

"With less remorse than Pyrrhus' bleeding sword

"Now falls on Priam.

"Get out, you strumpet, Fortune! All you gods,

"In general council ought to take away Fortune's power;

"You ought to break away all the spokes and the rim from her wheel,

"And bowl the wheel's round hub down the hill of Heaven,

"As low as to the fiends!"

Polonius said, "This is too long."

Hamlet replied, "It shall go to the barber's to be cut, along with your beard."

Hamlet then said to the first actor, "Please, continue. This critic here prefers dancing and singing or a bawdy tale, or else he falls asleep. Continue. Recite the part about Hecuba."

Hecuba was Priam's wife, the Queen of Troy. She had bore many sons to him, including Hector, the Crown Prince of Troy, whom she had witnessed Achilles killing. Following the fall of Troy, she was made a slave woman, and according to some accounts, she went insane.

The first actor recited this line:

"*But who, oh, who had seen the mobled Queen —*"

Hamlet asked, "The mobled Queen?"

The word "mobled," which was little used, meant "muffled." Hecuba's face was muffled.

"That's a good word," Polonius said. "'Mobled Queen' is good."

The first actor continued,

"*Runs barefoot up and down, threatening the flames*

"*With blinding tears; a rag upon that head*

"*Where recently a crown had stood, and for a robe,*

"*About her thin and totally exhausted-by-excessive-childbirth loins,*

"*A blanket, which she in the alarm of fear had caught up.*

"*Any person who had seen Hecuba in this state, with bitter words*

"*Would have railed treasonously against Lady Fortune's rule.*

"*But if the gods themselves had seen her*

"*When she saw Pyrrhus make malicious sport*

"*By chopping with his sword her husband's limbs,*

"*The instant burst of clamor that she made,*

"*Unless mortal troubles move them not at all,*

"*Would have made tearful the burning eyes — the stars — of Heaven,*

"*And would have brought sympathetic suffering to the gods.*"

Polonius said to Hamlet, "Look, the actor's face has changed color — it is pale — and he has tears in his eyes. Please, let us hear no more."

"Very good," Hamlet said to the first actor. "I'll have you speak the rest of the speech soon."

Hamlet then said to Polonius, "My good lord, will you see that the actors are well accommodated? Listen to me. Let them be well treated because they are the summary and brief chronicles of the time. It would be better for you to have a bad epitaph after you die than their ill will while you live."

"My lord, I will treat them according to their desert."

"By God, man, treat them better than that!" Hamlet said. "If you treat people according to what they deserve, who would escape being whipped? Treat them according to your own honor and dignity. The less they deserve, the more merit is in your generosity to them. Take them to their quarters."

Hamlet's "insanity" involved his being very rude to others, but he wanted the actors to be well taken of.

"Come, sirs," Polonius said to the actors.

"Follow him, friends," Hamlet said. "We'll have a play tomorrow."

Polonius and all the actors began to leave, but Hamlet began to speak to the first actor, so Polonius and all the other actors stopped at the door.

Hamlet said to the first actor, "Listen to me, old friend. Can you and the other actors play the *Murder of Gonzago?*"

"Yes, my lord."

"We'll have that tomorrow night," Hamlet said. "You could, if I asked you to, memorize a speech of some dozen or sixteen lines, which I would write and insert in the play, couldn't you?"

"Yes, my lord."

"Very good," Hamlet said. "Follow that lord, whose name is Polonius, and don't make fun of him."

Polonius and the actors departed.

Hamlet said to Rosencrantz and Guildenstern, who had quietly listened to the recitation of the poetry, "My good friends, I'll leave you until tonight. You are welcome to Elsinore."

"Thank you, my good lord," Rosencrantz said.

"May God be with you," Hamlet replied.

Rosencrantz and Guildenstern departed.

"Now I am alone," Hamlet said to himself. "Oh, what a rogue and peasant slave am I! Is it not monstrous that this actor here, performing what is only a fiction, a dream, and a pretense — not the reality — of suffering, could force his inner being to be so in harmony with his acting that he could make his face turn pale, bring tears to his eyes, make his entire body seem to be suffering with grief, make his voice broken, and use his whole being to serve his acting. And all for nothing that actually affects him! He did all this for Hecuba! What is Hecuba to him, or he to Hecuba, that he should weep for her? What would he do, if he had the motive and the cue for suffering that I have? My uncle, who has married my mother, has murdered my father! This actor would drown the stage with tears and burst everyone's ears with horrifying speeches. He would make the guilty insane, horrify the innocent, astonish the ignorant, and bewilder everyone's eyes and ears.

"Yet I, who am a dull and muddy-spirited rascal, mope, like John the daydreamer, not stirred to action by my cause and unable to say anything. I can do or speak nothing, no, not for a King, upon whose property and most dear life damned destruction was made.

"Am I a coward? Who calls me villain? Who breaks my head? Who plucks hairs from my beard, and blows them in my face? Who tweaks me by the nose? Who tells me that I lie in my throat as deep as to the lungs? Who does these things to me? Ha!

"By God, I should swallow these insults. I must have the anger of a pigeon, and I must lack the courage that would make me resent such bitter oppression, or else by now I would have fed the slave's offal to the kites — birds of prey — and made them fat. The slave I mean is King Claudius — that bloody, bawdy villain! He is a remorseless, treacherous, lecherous, unnatural villain! Oh, vengeance!

"Why, what an ass am I! This is most brave, that I, the son of a dear father who has been murdered, prompted by Heaven and Hell to seek my revenge, must, like a whore, unpack my heart with words, and curse, exactly like a prostitute or a lowly kitchen scullion! Damn!

"Get busy, my brain, and think of a plan!

"I have heard that guilty creatures sitting at a play have by the artistry of the scene been so struck to the soul that they have immediately confessed their evil deeds and crimes. Murder, although it has no tongue, will speak very miraculously — murder will out! I'll have these actors perform a play with a plot something like the murder of my father with my uncle as a member of the audience. I'll observe his looks; I'll probe him deeply — to the quick. If he flinches, I will know my course of action. I will know what I should do.

"The spirit — the ghost that claims to be my father — that I have seen may be the Devil in disguise. The Devil has the power to assume a pleasing shape. Perhaps, because my spirit is weak and melancholy — and the Devil can powerfully influence people who have such moods — he is deluding me so that I will do something that will make me damned.

"I need more substantial evidence than what I have received from the ghost. I can get such evidence by watching my uncle as he watches the play. The play is the thing whereby I'll learn the conscience of the King."

CHAPTER 3

— 3.1 —

In a room of the castle, King Claudius, Queen Gertrude, Polonius, Ophelia, Rosencrantz, and Guildenstern were meeting the following day.

King Claudius asked Rosencrantz and Guildenstern, "Can't you, by having conversations with Hamlet, learn from him why he is putting on and assuming this mental confusion and grating so harshly all his days of quiet with turbulent and dangerous lunacy?"

King Claudius was growing suspicious that perhaps Hamlet's insanity was not real, but just an act.

"He confesses that he feels mentally confused," Rosencrantz said, "but he will not say from what cause."

"Also, we do not find that he is willing to be questioned," Guildenstern said. "Instead, with a crafty madness, he keeps himself aloof and will not answer our questions when we try to have him make some confession about how he truly feels."

"Did he receive and welcome you well?" Queen Gertrude asked.

"He was exactly like a gentleman," Rosencrantz said.

"But he had to force himself to be welcoming," Guildenstern said.

"He did not ask questions, but he freely answered our questions," Rosencrantz said.

Rosencrantz was contradicting what Guildenstern had said just a little earlier. He was hoping not to have to reveal that Hamlet had found out that the King and Queen had sent for Guildenstern and him. He did not want the King and Queen to ask what questions Hamlet had asked Guildenstern and him.

"Did you persuade him to engage in any entertainment?" Queen Gertrude asked.

"Madam, it so happened that we overtook and passed certain actors as we traveled here. We told him about these actors, and he seemed joyful to hear about them. They are here in the castle, and I believe that they already have his orders to perform a play for him tonight."

"That is true," Polonius said. "Hamlet asked me to entreat your majesties to hear and see the play."

"I will with all my heart," King Claudius said, "and I am happy to hear that Hamlet wants to see a play. Rosencrantz and Guildenstern, you good gentlemen, give him further encouragement and stimulate his desire to engage in such entertainments."

"We shall, my lord," Rosencrantz said.

Rosencrantz and Guildenstern left the room.

"Sweet Gertrude, leave us, also," King Claudius said. "We have privately sent for Hamlet to come here so that, as if it were by accident, he may here come face to face with Ophelia. Her father and I, lawful spies, will hide ourselves so that, seeing them while we ourselves are unseen, we may frankly judge their encounter and learn from Hamlet's behavior whether the affliction of his love for her is or is not the cause of his mental disturbance."

"I shall obey you," Queen Gertrude said to King Claudius.

She added, "Ophelia, I hope and wish that your beauty and charms are the happy cause of Hamlet's wildness. I also hope that your virtues will bring him around to his usual self again, to both his and your benefit."

"Madam, I hope that Hamlet returns to his usual self," Ophelia replied.

Queen Gertrude left the room.

Ophelia's father, Polonius, said, "Ophelia, walk over here."

He then said to King Claudius, "Gracious majesty, if it so please you, we will hide ourselves."

He gave a book to Ophelia and said, "Take this religious book and read it so that you have an excuse for being alone. We are often to blame in this — it has been found to be true — that with the appearance of devotion and pious behavior we do sugar over — hide — the work of the Devil himself."

Polonius meant that they were using a religious book in an act of deception; the book would assist Polonius and King Claudius in spying on Hamlet when he thought that he was talking privately to Ophelia.

King Claudius heard Polonius' words and thought, *His words are too true! How painful a whipping that speech gives my conscience! The harlot's cheek, beautified with plastered-on cosmetics, is not uglier to the thing that beautifies it than is my deed to my most painted — hypocritical — words. This is a heavy burden! The whore disguises her ugliness with makeup, and I disguise my ugly sin with pretty but hypocritical words. My conscience is guilty.*

Polonius said, "I hear Hamlet coming. Let us hide ourselves, my lord."

They hid behind an arras: a wall hanging.

Of course, Hamlet could not hear King Claudius' thoughts, but they helped confirm what the ghost had told Hamlet.

Ophelia remained in the room, but Hamlet did not see her at first.

Hamlet entered the room and said, "To be, or not to be: That is the question. To exist or not to exist. Is it nobler in the mind to suffer the missiles and arrows of outrageous fortune, or to take arms against a sea of troubles, and by opposing them end them?"

To take up arms — weapons — to fight a sea is futile. Using weapons to fight a sea of troubles may be useless — unless the weapons are used to end one's own life, thereby ending one's troubles.

Hamlet was asking which course was better to take: Is it better to commit suicide or to endure a life of troubles?

"To die is to sleep; it is no more than that. If by sleeping we could end the heartache and the thousand natural shocks such as pain and illness that flesh is heir to, then that would be a consummation — an end — that we could devoutly wish for.

"To die is to sleep. To sleep is perhaps to dream. This is an obstacle because in that sleep of death what dreams may come to us after we have shuffled off and gotten free from this mortal coil, this business of humanity? Those dreams must make us hesitate and think before ending this life. Those dreams are why we endure unhappiness during a long life. Who would bear the whips and scorns of time, the wrongs inflicted on us by an oppressor, insulting treatment by proud men, the pangs of unrequited love, the delay and ineffectiveness of the law, the insolence of those who hold office, and the spurns given to those of patient merit by those who are unworthy? Who would bear these insults when he could secure his release from life with a mere dagger? Who would bear burdens, and grunt and sweat under a weary life, except that the dread of something after death, the unknown country from whose bourn no traveller returns to live his life, confounds and bewilders our will and makes us prefer to bear those ills we have instead of flying to others that we know not of?

"Thus conscience makes cowards of us all, and thus the natural color of resolution is covered over with the sickly and pale cast of thought about the evil things that may come to us after we die. And so enterprises of great gravity and importance turn awry because of these thoughts and so these enterprises of great gravity are never carried out."

Hamlet saw Ophelia and said to himself, "But I must stop my private reflections now."

He said out loud, "The fair and beautiful Ophelia! Nymph, in your prayers be sure to remember all my sins."

"My good lord, how have you been for all this long time?"

"I humbly thank you for asking," Hamlet said. "I have been well, well, well."

"My lord, I have remembrances of yours that I have longed for a long time to give back to you. Please, take them back now."

"No, not I," Hamlet replied, "I never gave you anything."

He thought, *I am much different from the man who gave you those remembrances.*

"My honored lord, you know very well you gave me these remembrances, and when you gave them to me you spoke perfumed words of such sweet breath that they made the things richer. Now that their perfume is lost, take these remembrances back because to the noble mind rich gifts grow poor when givers prove unkind."

Certainly, Hamlet in his "madness" had been unkind recently, especially to Ophelia's father.

Ophelia handed Hamlet some letters and said, "There, my lord."

Hamlet asked, "Do you mean that? Are you honest? And are you chaste?"

"My lord!"

"Are you fair and beautiful?"

"What does your lordship mean?"

"I mean that if you are chaste and beautiful, your chastity should permit no approach to your beauty. Your chastity should protect your beauty. Women are vulnerable because of their beauty."

"Could beauty, my lord, have better commerce — a better relationship or association — than with chastity?"

"Yes, it can," Hamlet said. "The power of beauty can transform honesty from what it is to a bawd — a prostitute. This power of beauty is stronger than the power of chastity to make beauty chaste. At one time, this was a paradox, but now our times have shown that it is true. Beauty is likely to make a chaste woman a whore. Virtue by itself is unlikely to keep a beautiful woman chaste."

Hamlet hesitated. He may have thought about his mother.

He then said, "I loved you once."

"Indeed, my lord, you made me believe so."

"You should not have believed me. Virtue, grafted onto our nature — which comes from that old sinner named Adam — cannot change our nature so much that we do not relish sin."

He hesitated again and then said, "I did not really love you."

"I was all the more deceived," Ophelia replied.

"Get you to a nunnery," Hamlet said. "Why would you want to be a breeder of sinners?"

Hamlet wanted Ophelia to become a nun and never to bear children. In his present mood, he wanted Humankind to die out, and one way for it to die out was for women to stop giving birth. The word "nunnery" was slang for brothel, but Hamlet was not using the word in that sense — he did not want Ophelia to do anything that could result in the continuation of the human species.

Hamlet continued, "I am myself decent enough, but yet I could accuse myself of such things that it would have been better if my mother had not given birth to me. I am very proud, revengeful, and ambitious. I have more sins ready for me to commit than I have thoughts to put them in, imagination to give them shape, or time to act them in. What should such fellows as I am do while crawling between Earth and Heaven? We are arrant knaves, all of us; believe none of us. Go and live in a nunnery."

He stopped and then asked, "Where's your father?"

"At home, my lord."

"Let the doors stay shut against him, so that he may play the fool nowhere but in his own house. Farewell."

Ophelia prayed for Hamlet: "Oh, help him, you sweet Heavens!"

Hamlet said to her, "If you do marry, I'll give you this curse for your dowry. Even if you are as chaste as ice and as pure as snow, you shall not escape gossip and slander. You shall have a bad reputation. Get you to a nunnery, go. Farewell.

"Or, if you must marry, marry a fool; for wise men know well enough what monsters — horned cuckolds — you make of them. To a nunnery, go, and quickly, too. Farewell."

Ophelia prayed, "Heavenly powers, restore him to sanity!"

"I have heard much about your paintings, too," Hamlet said.

He was referring to the use of cosmetics that women "painted" on their faces.

"God has given you women one face, and you make yourselves another. You jig, you amble, and you lisp, and you call God's creatures by the wrong name — a chaste woman becomes a whore, and a husband becomes a cuckold — and you pretend that you do wanton acts out of ignorance.

"Whatever. I'll speak no more about it; it has made me mad. I say, we will have no more marriages. Those who are married already — all but one couple — shall live and continue to be married couples. The rest shall stay as they are and remain single. To a nunnery, go."

The one couple was King Claudius and Queen Gertrude.

Hamlet stormed off.

Ophelia said, "Oh, what a noble mind is here overthrown by madness! The courtier's, soldier's, scholar's eye, tongue, sword are overthrown. The expectancy and rose — our finest hope and the apparent heir to the throne — of our fair state are overthrown. The mirror of attractiveness and the pattern of perfect behavior are overthrown. The observed of all observers — the honored and respected object of every courtier — is quite, quite overthrown!

"And I, of ladies most dejected and wretched, who sucked the honey of his musical vows, see that noble and most sovereign reason that used to formerly jangle like sweet bells is now out of tune and harsh. I see that his unmatched form and feature in the full flower of his youth has been blasted by madness.

"I am filled with sorrow because I have seen what I have seen, and because I see what I see!"

King Claudius and Polonius came out of hiding.

"Love?" King Claudius said. "Hamlet's emotions do not incline that way. In addition, the things that he said, although they lacked form a little, did not sound mad. There is something in Hamlet's soul, over which his melancholy sits on brood the way a bird sits on eggs, and I suspect that what will hatch and be disclosed will be something dangerous. To prevent that danger, I have just now decided to send Hamlet to England. There he shall demand the tribute that England has not sent to Denmark. Perhaps the seas and different countries with various sights will expel this thing, whatever it is, that is in his heart and has bothered his brain so much that it makes him unlike his usual self."

King Claudius asked Polonius, "What is your opinion? What do you think?"

"Your plan is good," Polonius replied, "but I still believe that the origin and commencement of his grief has sprung from rejected love."

Polonius said to his daughter, "How are you, Ophelia? You need not tell us what Lord Hamlet said: We heard everything."

He then said to King Claudius, "My lord, do as you please; however, if you think it fit, after the play let the Queen his mother be alone with him to entreat him to reveal his grief. Let her be outspoken with him, and I'll be hidden, if it pleases you, where I can hear their conversation. If she does not find out what is the matter with him, then send him to England, or confine him wherever your wisdom shall think best."

"We will do as you suggest," King Claudius said. "It shall be so. Madness in great ones must not unwatched go."

Hamlet talked with the actors in a hall in the castle and gave them advice on how to perform their roles. First, he talked about speaking the lines he had specially written for the play, but quickly he talked about acting in general.

"Speak the speech, please, as I recited it to you, trippingly on the tongue," he said. "If you speak it in a pompous oratorical style as so many actors do, I prefer that the town-crier speak my lines.

"Also, do not saw the air too much with your hand, like this," he said, making an overly dramatic gesture. "Instead, do everything moderately. In the very torrent, tempest, and, as I may say, whirlwind of passion, you must acquire and beget a temperance that may give it smoothness.

"I am offended to my soul when I hear a robust wig-wearing fellow tear a passion to tatters, to very rags, to split the ears of the groundlings, those audience members who buy the cheapest tickets and watch the play while standing up rather than while seated. For the most part, the groundlings are capable of nothing but inexplicable dumbshows and noise. I would have such a fellow whipped for overacting the role of the blustery character Termagant; such performances out-Herod Herod — that ranting and raving tyrant of old-fashioned plays. Please, avoid such overacting."

"Yes, your honor," the first actor replied.

"Do not be too tame either, but let your own discretion be your tutor. Use your own judgment. Suit the action to the words, and suit the words to the action. Remember this especially: Do not overstep the moderation of nature. Anything overdone goes against the purpose of acting, whose end, both at the beginning and now, was and is, to hold, as it were, a mirror up to nature. Acting should be a mirror to virtue and to vice, and acting should show things as they really are at the time. Acting should be a mirror to our aging world. A realistic statue will show the wrinkles of an aged man, and a play should show the wrinkles of an aged world.

"If acting is overdone, or if it falls short, even if it makes the ignorant and undiscerning laugh, it cannot but make the judicious grieve. The censure of one judicious man must in your allowance overweigh a whole theater filled with ignorant and undiscerning audience members.

"There are actors whom I have seen and have heard others praise, and that highly, not to say blasphemously, who, neither having the accent of Christians — ordinary decent people — nor the gait of Christian, pagan, or any other man, have so strutted and bellowed that I have thought that some of Nature's journeymen — not God — had made men and had not made them well. That is how abominably these bad actors imitated humanity."

"Sir, I hope that we have corrected that failing moderately well," the first actor said.

"Correct that fault entirely," Hamlet replied. "And let those who play your clowns speak no more than is set down for them — no ad-libbing. Some clowns will laugh in order to set on some quantity of barren spectators to laugh, too. These bad clowns do this even though, when they ad-lib, some necessary issue in the play needs to be addressed. Such behavior is villainous, and it shows a most pitiful ambition in the fool who does such things."

He then said to the actors, "Go and get yourselves ready to perform."

The actors left the room as Polonius, Rosencrantz, and Guildenstern entered it.

Hamlet asked Polonius, "How are you, my lord? Will the King watch this play?"

"Yes, and the Queen, too. They are ready to see it right away."

"Tell the actors to get ready quickly."

Polonius left to carry out his errand.

Hamlet asked Rosencrantz and Guildenstern, "Will you two help to hasten the actors?"

"We will, my lord," Rosencrantz said.

Rosencrantz and Guildenstern left the room.

Hamlet called, "Horatio!"

Horatio walked into the room and said, "Here, sweet lord. I am at your service."

"Horatio, you are as well-adjusted a man as I have talked to and dealt with."

"Oh, my dear lord!"

"No, do not think that I am flattering you," Hamlet said, "for what advancement may I hope to receive from you, who have no revenue but your good spirits to feed and clothe you?

"Why should anyone flatter the poor? No, let the candied tongue lick absurd pomp the way that a fawning dog licks its master's hand or face. Let people bend the ready hinges of their knees to rich and powerful people so that profit may follow fawning. Do you understand me?

"Ever since my dear soul has been able to make choices and to distinguish between and evaluate men, she has chosen to be friends with you. You have been a person who has suffered — experienced — everything, and yet you have suffered — been harmed by — nothing. You are a man who has taken Lady Fortune's buffets and rewards with equal thanks. Blessed are those whose blood and judgment are so well commingled. Such people are not a pipe for Lady Fortune's finger to sound what note she please. You are not at her mercy; she cannot make you exuberant or miserable; you keep a steady head no matter what because you are not the slave of our emotions. Such men I hold in my heart of hearts — I hold you in my heart of hearts. But I am rambling on about this.

"King Claudius will see a play tonight. One scene of it depicts almost exactly the circumstances that I have told you of my father's death.

"Please, when that scene is being acted, use your senses to closely examine my uncle. We will get that fox out of his kennel. If his hidden guilt does not reveal itself when the actors recite a speech that I have written, then it is a damned ghost from Hell that we have seen, and those things I have imagined are as foul as the workshop of the blacksmith god: Vulcan.

"Observe him very carefully, and I will rivet my own eyes on his face. Afterward, we will compare what we have seen and concluded. We will decide whether he is guilty or innocent of the murder of my father."

"I will, my lord," Horatio said. "If he gets away with anything while this play is playing, I will answer for it."

Hamlet heard people approaching, so he said, "They are coming to the play; I must be empty-headed and play the fool now. Find yourself a place where you can observe my uncle's face."

King Claudius, Queen Gertrude, Polonius, Ophelia, Rosencrantz, Guildenstern, and others entered the hall. Some members of the King's Guard were carrying torches to provide light.

"How fares our kinsman Hamlet?" King Claudius asked.

By "fares," King Claudius meant "does," but "fare" can mean "food" and Hamlet deliberately misinterpreted "fares" as "dines."

"Excellently, truly," Hamlet replied. "My fare is the fare of the chameleon, which is thought to live on air. I eat the air, which is crammed with promises. You cannot feed capons — castrated cocks that are fattened to serve as food — with air and promises."

Hamlet was saying that he was being fed with promises; Hamlet was not King of Denmark — all he had was King Claudius' recommendation that Hamlet become King after Claudius died.

"This answer does not answer my question, Hamlet," King Claudius said. "These words are not for me — they are not mine."

"No, nor mine now," Hamlet said.

He meant that since he had released the words into the air, they no longer belonged to him.

Hamlet asked Polonius, "My lord, you acted once in the university, didn't you say?"

"That I did, my lord; and I was thought to be a good actor."

"What role did you play?"

"I played the role of Julius Caesar. I was killed in the Capitol; Brutus killed me."

"It was a brute part of him to kill so capital a calf there."

As usual, Hamlet was insulting Polonius. A "calf" was a fool.

Hamlet asked, "Are the actors ready?"

"Yes, my lord," Rosencrantz said. "They are ready when you are."

"Come here, my dear Hamlet, and sit by me," Queen Gertrude said.

"No, good mother, here's metal more attractive," Hamlet said, referring to Ophelia.

He was referring to Ophelia as if she were a magnet that was attracting him.

Polonius said to King Claudius, "Did you hear that?"

Hamlet did not want to sit by his mother because he wanted a clear view of King Claudius' face during the play. If he had sat by his mother, she would have been between him and the King.

Hamlet said to Ophelia, "Lady, shall I lie in your lap?"

As usual, the "mad" Hamlet was rude to Ophelia. "Lie in your lap" could be understood as "have sex with you in the missionary position."

Ophelia understood that meaning of Hamlet's words, and she replied, "No, my lord."

Hamlet said, "I mean, may I lie with my head upon your lap?"

Ophelia replied, "Yes, my lord."

Hamlet asked her, "Did you think I meant country matters?"

The phrase "country matters" refers to sex. Sex is common among animals on a farm. When Hamlet said "country matters," he stressed the first syllable of "country."

"I thought nothing, my lord."

"That's a fair thought to lie between maidens' legs," Hamlet said.

"What is, my lord?"

"Nothing."

"Nothing" is "no thing." A penis is a thing, and a maiden has no thing between her legs. Nothing is also a zero, and a zero is an O, and an "O" is a symbol for what lies between a maiden's legs.

Ophelia, who understood what Hamlet was saying, said to him, "You are merry, my lord."

"Who, I?"

"Yes, my lord."

"Oh, God, I am your only joke-maker. What should a man do but be merry? Look at how cheerful my mother looks, and my father died not even two hours ago."

"Your father died four months ago, my lord."

"As long ago as that?" Hamlet said. "Let the Devil wear black, and I will have a suit of sables."

According to Hamlet's society, the Devil is black. Hamlet was joking again. Hamlet would give the Devil his black mourning clothes because Hamlet's father had died four months ago, which Hamlet was pretending to be a long time and so Hamlet would no longer need black mourning clothes. Hamlet would replace the black mourning clothes with sable furs — but since "sable" as a heraldic term means "black," he would still be wearing the color of mourning.

Hamlet continued, "Oh, Heavens! My father died two months ago, and he has not been forgotten yet? Then there is hope that the memory of a great man may outlive his life by half a year, but, by the Virgin Mary, he must build churches to keep his memory alive, or else he shall be forgotten just like the hobby-horse, about which this lyric is sung: '*For, oh, for, oh, the hobby-horse is forgotten.*'"

Trumpets sounded, and the actors performed a dumbshow — they pantomimed part of the play that was to follow:

An Actor-King and an Actor-Queen who were very loving walked to the acting area. The Queen embraced the King, and he embraced her. She knelt and made a show of protestations of love to him. He helped her stand up, and he rested his head on her neck. He then lay down upon a bank of flowers and fell asleep. She, seeing him asleep, left him. Immediately came in a fellow who took off the King's crown, kissed it, and then poured poison in the King's ears. The fellow exited. The Queen returned and found the King dead. She grieved passionately. The Poisoner, with some two or three others, came in again and pretended to lament with her. The dead body was carried away. The Poisoner wooed the Queen with gifts: She seemed loath and unwilling for awhile, but in the end she accepted his love.

The actors then exited.

"What is the meaning of this dumbshow, my lord?" Ophelia asked Hamlet.

"By the Virgin Mary, this is sneaking *mallecho*; *mallecho* means mischief," Hamlet replied.

Malhecho is Spanish for "mischief."

"Probably this dumbshow depicts the plot of the play," Ophelia said.

The Prologue — an actor who recited the prologue to the play, often telling the audience members its meaning — entered.

"We shall learn the plot of the play from this fellow," Hamlet said. "The actors cannot keep a secret; they'll tell everything."

"Will he tell us the meaning of this dumbshow we just saw?" Ophelia asked.

"Yes, or any show that you'll show him. If you are not ashamed to show him, he is not ashamed to tell you what it means."

Ophelia, who understood that Hamlet was talking about showing private parts, said to him, "You are wicked. You are wicked. I'll watch the play."

The Prologue said these few words:

"*For us, and for our tragedy,*

"*Here stooping to your clemency,*

"*We beg your hearing patiently.*"

Usually, play prologues are longer and more informative.

Hamlet asked, "Is this a prologue, or the posy of a ring?"

The posy of a ring is the words written on the inside of a finger ring. Here is an example: "Love me, and leave me not."

Ophelia said, "This prologue is brief, my lord."

"It is as brief as a woman's love," Hamlet said.

Two actors walked into the acting area. One actor played the "King," and the other actor played the "Queen."

The Actor-King recited these lines:

"Full thirty times has Phoebus' cart — the Sun — gone round

"Neptune's salt wash — the Ocean — and Tellus' orbed ground — the Earth,

"And thirty dozen moons with borrowed light from the Sun

"About the world have times twelve thirties been,

"Since love our hearts and Hymen did our hands

"Unite mutually in most sacred bonds."

Hamlet thought, *This is an old-fashioned play. It has many references to mythology. Neptune is the Roman god of the sea, Tellus is a Roman Earth goddess, and Hymen is the Roman god of marriage.*

This play uses an elevated style of language. All the playwright is trying to say here is that this King and Queen have been married for thirty years. However, the playwright does not use elevated language well. Attempts to use elevated and fancy language sometimes result in bad writing.

The Actor-Queen recited these lines:

"So many journeys may the Sun and Moon

"Make us again count over before our love is done!

"Let us live our married life for another thirty years!

"But, woe is me, you are so sick lately,

"So far from cheerfulness and from your former state,

"That I distrust your health. Yet, though I distrust it,

"Do not let that discomfort you, my lord,

"For women's fear and love holds quantity;

"In neither aught, or in extremity.

"Either there is none of either, or too much of both.

"Now, what my love is, experience has made you know;

"And as my love is measured, my fear is so.

"I love you much, so I worry much about your health.

"*Where love is great, the littlest doubts become fear;*
"*Where little fears grow great, great love grows there.*
"*The more I love you, the more I fear for you.*"
The Actor-King recited these lines:
"*Truly, I must leave you, love, and soon, too;*
"*My vital organs their functions cease to do:*
"*And you shall live in this fair world after I am dead,*
"*Honored, beloved; and perhaps one as kind*
"*For your new husband shall you —*"
The Actor-Queen interrupted by reciting these lines:
"*Oh, confound the rest!*
"*Such love must necessarily be treason in my breast:*
"*In a second marriage let me be accurst!*
"*None wed the second husband except those who killed the first.*"
Hamlet thought, *Wormwood, wormwood. This is bitter medicine. According to the Actor-Queen, when a widow remarries, it is as if she had killed her first husband.*

The Actor-Queen continued:
"*The motives that lead to a second marriage*
"*Are mean considerations of worldly advantages, but none of love:*
"*A second time I kill my first husband dead,*
"*When a second husband kisses me in bed.*"
The Actor-King recited these lines:
"*I do believe you think those things that now you speak;*
"*But what we decide to do are vows we often break —*
"*People change their minds.*
"*What we decide to do is but the slave to memory,*
"*Of violent birth, but poor validity.*
"*We can forget our vows;*
"*We strongly mean to keep them at first but then we forget.*
"*Vows now, like unripe fruit, stick on the tree;*
"*But they fall, unshaken,*
"*When they become mellow and lose their passion.*
"*Most necessary it is that we forget*
"*To pay ourselves what to ourselves is debt.*

"A vow to do something is a debt we owe to ourselves.
"What we vow to do we vow in the heat of passion.
"Once the passion is over, we forget the vow.
"The violent excess of either grief or joy
"Destroys the power to carry out the vow.
"Where joy most revels, grief does most lament.
"A person with the greatest capacity for joy also has the greatest capacity for grief.
"But grief turns to joy, and joy turns to grief, with little cause.
"This world is not for ever, nor is it strange
"That even our loves should with our fortunes change.
"For it is a question left us yet to prove,
"Whether love decides our fortune, or fortune decides our love.
"When the great man's fortunes decline, you will see his best friend flee from him;
"When a poor man's fortune improves, he makes friends out of former enemies.
"And therefore does friendship on fortune tend;
"For a man who does not need anything shall never lack a friend,
"But when a man who is in need seeks help from a hollow, insincere friend,
"The needy man turns his hollow, insincere friend into his enemy.
"But, to end orderly where I had begun,
"Our desires and destinies do so contrary run
"That our plans and designs always are overthrown;
"Our thoughts are ours, their ends are none of our own:
"So you think you will no second husband wed,
"But your thoughts will die when your first husband is dead."
The Actor-Queen recited these lines:
"May Earth not give food to me, nor Heaven light!
"May entertainment and sleep stay away from me both day and night!
"May to desperation turn my trust and hope!
"May a hermit's life in prison be all I ask for and receive!
"May everything that brings joy
"Meet an opponent who can these things destroy.
"May everything both here and hereafter — in this life and in the afterlife — bring me lasting strife,

"If, once I am a widow, I ever again become a wife!"

Hamlet thought, *How could she break her promise now, after saying these words?*

The Actor-King recited these lines:

"You have sworn deeply. Sweet, leave me here awhile.

"My spirits grow dull, and I would like to beguile

"The tedious day with sleep."

He fell asleep.

The Actor-Queen recited these lines:

"May sleep rock gently and soothe your brain,

"And may ill fortune never come between us twain!"

The Actor-Queen exited.

Hamlet ask his mother, "Madam, how do you like this play?"

Queen Gertrude replied, "The lady protests too much, I think. Too much protesting makes the content of her words suspected."

"Oh, but I am sure that she'll keep her word," Hamlet lied.

King Claudius asked Hamlet, "Do you know the plot of the play? Is there any offence in it?"

By "offense," King Claudius meant "anything offensive," but Hamlet deliberately misinterpreted the word "offense" to mean "crime."

"No, no, the actors are only jesting; they are poisoning in jest — it is all make believe. There is no offence in the world."

"What is the title of this play??"

"*The Mousetrap*," Hamlet replied. "By the Virgin Mary, how did it get its name? Tropically."

He thought, *"Tropically" means "figuratively." A trope is a figure of speech, and the play is figuratively a trap that I have set for King Claudius. Perhaps I should have used this word: "Trapically."*

Hamlet added, "This play depicts a real-life murder committed in Vienna. Gonzago is the Duke's name; his wife's name is Baptista. You shall see this soon enough. It is a knavish piece of work, but so what? As for your majesty and we who have free souls, this play is not about us. Let the guilty wince and kick like a horse whose saddle sore is stung; all of us are innocent."

An actor playing the role of Lucianus entered.

Hamlet said, "This is Lucianus, the King's nephew."

Ophelia said to him, "You are as good as a chorus that explains everything, my lord."

"I could provide commentary on what happens between you and your lover," Hamlet replied. "I could be like the guy who narrates a puppet show if I saw your puppet and your lover's puppet having intercourse."

"You are keen, my lord, you are keen," Ophelia said.

By "keen," she meant "sharp."

Hamlet replied, "It would cost you a groaning to take off my edge."

"Edge" could mean "sharp edge of a knife," but Hamlet used "edge" with its meaning of "sharp sexual desire."

If Ophelia were to take off Hamlet's edge, she would groan during the pain of breaking her hymen and later she would groan as she gave birth.

Ophelia commented, "Always better, and worse."

She meant that Hamlet's responses to her were wittier — and more offensive — than her comments to him.

Having in mind that brides promised in the marriage ceremony to take their husbands for better or for worse, Hamlet replied, "So you women mis-take your husbands."

Women mis-take their husbands when they do not keep their vows, and when they substitute one husband for another.

He then said to the actor, "Begin, murderer; stop making your damnable faces, and begin. Come: *The croaking raven does bellow for revenge.*"

Hamlet was misquoting — perhaps deliberately — two lines from the play *The True Tragedy of Richard III*: "The screeching raven sits croaking for revenge / Whole herds of beasts come bellowing for revenge."

The actor playing Lucianus said these lines:

"*Thoughts evil and black, hands apt, poison, and a time suitable;*

"*Opportunity perfect, with no creature seeing;*

"*You mixture rank and poisonous, made of weeds collected and combined at midnight,*

"*Three times blasted with the bane of the goddess of witchcraft, Hecate,*

"*Your natural magic and dire property*

"*Do usurp and kill wholesome life immediately.*"

The actor playing Lucianus poured the poison into the ears of the Actor-King.

Hamlet said, "He is poisoning him in the garden for his estate. His name's Gonzago. The story is popular, and it is written in good Italian. You shall see soon how the murderer gets the love of Gonzago's wife."

Ophelia said, "The King rises. He is standing up."

"What, is he frightened by false fire!" Hamlet asked. "Is he frightened by the firing of a gun loaded with blanks? Is he frightened by a mere play?"

"How are you, my lord?" Queen Gertrude asked.

"Stop the play!" Polonius ordered.

"Get me some light so I can leave!" King Claudius ordered.

People shouted, "Lights, lights, lights!"

Members of the King's Guard stepped forward with their torches.

Everyone except Hamlet and Horatio left the hall.

Hamlet was in a giddy mood. He had watched King Claudius closely during the play and had reached a decision about whether the King was guilty of the murder of Hamlet's father.

Hamlet sang these verses to Horatio, who had also watched King Claudius closely during the play:

"*Why, let the wounded deer go weep,*

"*The hart, unhurt, play;*

"*For some must stay awake, while some must sleep:*

"*So runs the world always.*"

Hamlet then said, "Would not the success of this play, sir, and a forest of feathers — if the rest of my fortunes turn Turk and run against me — with two Provincial roses, aka large rosettes, on my razed, slashed-in-accordance-with-fashion, shoes, get me a fellowship in a cry — a pack — of players, sir? A successful play and the appropriate costume should get me a share of the profits in a company of actors."

Actors of the time wore many feathers as part of their costumes. Rosettes were worn on the shoes; they hid the ties of the shoes. Razed shoes were fashionable shoes that had been slashed and inlaid with different colored silks and that were then stitched and perhaps embroidered.

"Those things might get you half a share," Horatio said.

"A whole share is what I would get," Hamlet replied.

He then sang these extempore — just now made up — verses:

"*For you do know, this realm was deprived, oh, Damon dear,*

"Of Jove himself, the King of gods and men past;

"And now reigns here

"A very, very — pajock."

The song was about Hamlet's father, whose murder had deprived Denmark of its rightful King. "Damon" was a traditional name in pastoral poetry for a shepherd. A "pajock" was an unusual word that meant "a base and contemptible fellow."

Horatio said, "You might have rhymed."

The rhyme would have been with "past": ass.

"Oh, good Horatio," Hamlet said. "I will bet a thousand pounds that the ghost spoke the truth. Did you notice King Claudius' face?"

"Very well, my lord."

"Did you see how he reacted to the talk about the poisoning?"

"I watched him very closely, my lord."

"Ah, ha!" Hamlet, still giddy from the success of the trap, said.

He shouted, "Come, let's have some music! Come, bring the flute-like recorders!"

He sang these verses:

"For if the King likes not the comedy,

"Why then, belike, he likes it not, perdy."

The word *"perdy"* was colloquial for *"par dieu,"* which is French for "By God."

Hamlet shouted, "Come, bring some music!"

Rosencrantz and Guildenstern entered the hall.

"My good lord, may I have a word with you?" Guildenstern asked.

"Sir, you may have as many words as would fill a whole history," Hamlet replied.

"The King, sir —" Guildenstern began.

Hamlet interrupted: "Yes, sir, what about him?"

"— is in his private chamber now; he is very much not his usual self."

"Is he drunk?" Hamlet asked.

"No, my lord," Guildenstern said. "He is angry. He is filled with choler."

"You should know to tell this to a doctor, not to me," Hamlet said. "If I were to be his doctor, I would purge him, and his purgation might make him angrier."

Hamlet's society existed before the age of modern medicine. Doctors in Hamlet's society believed that the human body had four humors, or vital fluids. Each humor made a contribution to the personality, and for a human being to be sane and healthy, the four humors had to be present in the right amounts. If a man had too much of a certain humor, it would harm his personality and health.

Blood was the sanguine humor. A sanguine man was optimistic.

Phlegm was the phlegmatic humor. A phlegmatic man was calm.

Yellow bile was the choleric humor. A choleric man was angry.

Black bile was the melancholic humor. A melancholic man was gloomy.

When a man was ill, doctors would try to get the four humors back into balance by purging him, often through bloodletting or through the use of laxatives.

When Hamlet talked about purging King Claudius, he meant using his sword to purge so much of the King's blood that the King would die.

Another type of purgation was purging one's sins through prayer and confession, but Hamlet wanted King Claudius to suffer for his sins, not be purged of them.

"My good lord," Guildenstern replied, "talk sense to me and do not wildly run away from the topic of discussion."

"I am tame, sir," Hamlet said. "Tell me what you have to tell me."

"The Queen, your mother, whose spirit is greatly afflicted, has sent me to you."

"You are welcome."

"My good lord," Guildenstern said, "your courteous words are not of the right kind. You need to listen to me and to make serious answers. If you are willing to give me a serious answer, then I will do your mother's errand and give you the message that she wanted me to give you. If you are not willing to give me a serious answer, then I will ask for your permission to leave and I will return to your mother, and you and I need not have any other conversation."

"Sir, I cannot."

"Cannot what, my lord?" Rosencrantz said.

"Make you a serious answer. My intelligence is diseased; however, sir, such answer as I can make, you shall get — or rather, as you say, my mother shall get. Therefore, let's have no longer delay, but instead let's get to the point. My mother, you say —"

"This is what she says," Rosencrantz replied. "She says that your behavior has amazed and astonished her."

"Oh, what a wonderful son, who can so astonish a mother!" Hamlet said. "But is there no sequel at the heels of this mother's admiration? What else did she say? Tell me."

"She wants to speak with you in her private chamber, before you go to bed," Rosencrantz replied.

"We shall obey even if she were ten times our mother. Have you any further trade with us?" Hamlet said.

Rosencrantz and Guildenstern had once been Hamlet's friends, but he did not now regard them as his friends. Hamlet realized that they were loyal to King Claudius, not to him. Therefore, Hamlet used the royal plural to let them know that he no longer wished to continue this topic of conversation. He also contemptuously used the word "trade," which meant "business."

"My lord, you once were friends with me," Rosencrantz said.

"And I still am," Hamlet lied, "by these pickers and stealers."

The "pickers and stealers" were his fingers. The Catechism in the Book of Common Prayer has this vow that the catechumen makes: "To keep my hands from picking and stealing." The word "picking" in this context means "pilfering."

"My good lord, what is your cause of distemper?" Rosencrantz asked. "You do, surely, bar the door upon your own liberty, if you will not tell your griefs to your friends. Your mind would be healthier and freer if only you would tell your troubles to your friends."

"Sir, I lack advancement," Hamlet replied.

Earlier, after Hamlet had called Denmark his prison, Rosencrantz and Guildenstern had suggested that Hamlet's ambition — to be King — had made him feel that way. Hamlet had denied it.

"How can that be, when you have the voice of the King himself for your succession in Denmark?" Rosencrantz said. "King Claudius has stated publicly that he wants you to be King after he dies."

"Yes, but sir, 'While the grass grows' — the proverb is somewhat musty," Hamlet replied.

Hamlet meant that the proverb — while the grass grows, the horse starves — was so well known that he need not state all of it.

The actors, carrying recorders — musical instruments resembling flutes — entered the hall.

"Oh, the recorders!" Hamlet said.

He requested of an actor, "Let me see one."

He then said to Rosencrantz and Guildenstern, "Step over here so that I can have a few private words with you."

They went a little distance from the actors, and Hamlet asked them, "Why do you go about to recover — to gain — the wind of me, as if you would drive me into a toil?"

Hamlet was accusing them of trying to lead him into a trap. In doing so, he used hunting terminology. A hunter would recover the wind — that it, go upwind so that the animals being hunted would catch his scent and then move away from him toward the hunters who were waiting downwind and so could not be scented. The animals would walk into a toil — a trap — set by the hunters.

"Oh, my lord, if my duty be too bold, my friendship for you is too unmannerly," Guildenstern said.

He meant that his friendship and concern for Hamlet were responsible if he had seemed to have bad manners.

"I do not well understand that," Hamlet replied.

What he did not well understand was how Rosencrantz and Guildenstern could now say that they were his friends.

Hamlet asked Guildenstern, "Will you play upon this pipe — this recorder?"

"My lord, I cannot."

"Please."

"Believe me, I cannot."

"I beg you to."

"I do not know how to play it, my lord."

"It is as easy as lying," Hamlet said. "Cover these holes in the pipe with your fingers and thumb, and then give it breath with your mouth, and it will put forth most eloquent music. Look here, these are the holes."

"But I cannot use them to make anything resembling harmony," Guildenstern said. "I have not the skill."

"Why, see here," Hamlet said. "See how unworthily you are treating me! You want to play upon me; you seem to know my stops; you want to push my buttons and learn my secrets; you want to sound me from my lowest note to the top of my compass or range."

"Sound me" was a pun that meant both "play me and make me give forth sounds" and "probe or fathom me to find out what is hidden in my depths."

Hamlet continued, "Much music — excellent voice — is in this little instrument called the recorder, yet you cannot make it speak. Do you think I am easier to be played on than a pipe? Call me what instrument you will, although you can fret me, yet you cannot play upon me."

Again Hamlet was punning. "To fret" means "to irritate," and frets are the ridges on some stringed instruments that are used to produce notes.

Hamlet wanted Rosencrantz and Guildenstern to know that he would not allow their tricks to be successful with him.

Polonius entered the hall, and Hamlet said to him, "God bless you, sir!"

"My lord, the Queen wants to speak with you, and that immediately," Polonius said.

Hamlet replied, "Do you see yonder cloud that's almost in the shape of a camel?"

It was night, and they were inside the hall of the castle, but Polonius believed that Hamlet was insane and he did not want to upset him.

Polonius replied, "By the Mass, the cloud is like a camel, indeed."

"I think that it is like a weasel," Hamlet said.

"It has a back like a weasel," Polonius said.

The back of a camel and the back of a weasel are not similar.

"Or like a whale?" Hamlet asked.

"Very like a whale," Polonius replied.

"Then I will come to my mother by and by — soon."

He thought, *They play along with my fooling — my acting like a madman — to the top of my bent.*

The "top of a bent" is a term from archery. It means "the greatest extent that a bow can be bent."

Hamlet repeated, "I will come by and by."

"I will tell her that," Polonius said.

"'By and by' is easily said," Hamlet said.

Polonius left the hall.

Hamlet said to Rosencrantz and Guildenstern, "Leave me, friends."

They departed, leaving Hamlet alone.

Hamlet said to himself, "Now is the very witching time — the time when witches appear — of night, when churchyards yawn and Hell itself breathes out contagion upon this world. Now I could catch the contagion and drink hot blood and be tempted to commit murder and do such bitter business as the day would quake to look on.

"Be careful, Hamlet!

"Now I will go to my mother. Oh, heart, do not lose your natural feeling of love for your mother. Do not ever let the soul of Nero enter this firm bosom. Nero, Emperor of Rome, committed matricide — he had his own mother put to death.

"Let me be cruel, but not unnatural. I will speak daggers to my mother, but I will not use any daggers. My tongue and soul in this will be hypocrites; let my soul pretend to be more savage than it is, and let my tongue pronounce the words that will make me seem more savage than I am.

"I will rebuke her mightily with words, but I will not put into deeds what I say in words."

In a room in the castle, King Claudius talked with Rosencrantz and Guildenstern.

"I do not like the way that Hamlet is behaving," King Claudius said. "It is not safe for us to allow his madness free range. Therefore prepare yourselves to perform a commission I will give to you. Speedily I will give you a commission to go to England, and Hamlet shall go to England with you. The terms of our estate may not endure a hazard so dangerous as does hourly grow out of his lunacies. Hamlet's madness is a threat to me the King."

"We will make the necessary preparations," Guildenstern said. "It is a very holy and religious concern to want to keep safe the numerous subjects who depend upon your majesty. If something were to happen to you the King, it would have a bad effect upon your country and your subjects."

"An individual with one life is bound by natural law to use all its strength and intelligence to keep itself from harm," Rosencrantz said. "But much more bound is a spirit upon whose well-being the lives of many people depend and rest. A King does not die alone, but like a whirlpool, his death pulls with it what is near. It is like a massive wheel fixed on the summit of the highest mountain. To the wheel's huge spokes are fastened ten thousand lesser things. When the wheel falls down the mountain, each of the ten thousand lesser and petty things is harmed in the boisterous catastrophe. The general public groans when a King sighs. Never does a King sigh alone."

"Prepare yourselves to travel quickly," King Claudius said. "We will put fetters upon this fear, which now goes too free-footed. We will not allow Hamlet to roam freely in Denmark."

"We will hurry," Rosencrantz and Guildenstern said.

They exited as Polonius entered the room.

"My lord," Polonius said, "Hamlet is going to his mother's private chamber. Behind the arras I'll hide myself so I can hear their conversation. I am sure that she will berate him soundly.

"As you said, and wisely was it said, it is a good idea that someone other than a mother, since nature makes them partial to their sons, should listen to their conversation from a hidden spot."

Actually, hiding and listening to the conversation of Queen Gertrude and Hamlet had been Polonius' idea. He was flattering King Claudius by saying that the idea was the King's and that it was a wise plan.

Polonius said, "Fare you well, my liege. I'll call upon you before you go to bed and tell you what I learn."

"Thanks, my dear lord," King Claudius said.

Polonius exited, leaving King Claudius alone.

King Claudius said to himself, "My offence is so rank that it stinks to Heaven. It has the primal eldest curse upon it: a brother's murder — the murder of Abel by Cain. I cannot pray, although my desire to pray is as strong as my will and determination.

"My stronger guilt defeats my strong intent. And, like a man who has two tasks to do, I stand and pause as I consider which I shall first begin, and as I pause I neglect both tasks. I can pray and ask forgiveness of my sins and do what I can to make things right, or I can continue to pursue the path I am on and enjoy the fruits of my sin.

"So what if this cursed hand of mine is thicker than itself because it is coated with my brother's blood? Don't the sweet Heavens have enough rain to wash it as white as snow?"

King Claudius was thinking of part of Isaiah 1:18: "*Come now, and let us reason together, saith the Lord: though your sins be as scarlet, they shall be as white as snow; though they be red like crimson, they shall be as wool.*"

He continued, "What is the purpose of mercy except to confront the face of evil? Doesn't mercy forgive committed sins? And what's in prayer but this two-fold force: to pray for help to keep us from committing sins, and to pray for forgiveness of those sins we have committed."

King Claudius was thinking of Mathew 6:13: "*And lead us not into temptation, but deliver us from evil: For thine is the Kingdom, and the power, and the glory, for ever. Amen.*"

He continued, "I can look up; I have hope. I have committed the sin, and so I know what kind of prayer I must make. But what form of prayer can serve my turn? 'Forgive me my foul murder'? I cannot pray that because I still have the things for which I committed the murder: my crown, everything I was ambitious for, and my Queen. May one be pardoned and still keep the things that one acquired by committing the sin?

"In the corrupted currents of this world, a guilty hand that is coated with ill-gotten gold from committing a sin may shove aside justice. Often we see that parts of the spoils of a crime are used to bribe officials who ought to uphold the law, but it is not that way in Heaven. There, no one can avoid proper punishment. Here, no one can be forced to give evidence against himself. In Heaven, all evidence is revealed and we who are guilty are compelled to confess our sins and give the evidence that convicts us — we confess the bared teeth and frowning forehead of our faults.

"What then? What remains that I can do? I can see what repentance can do. What can repentance not do? But what can repentance do if one cannot repent?

"My state is wretched! My bosom is black as death! My soul has been caught, and as it struggles to be free, it is caught more firmly!

"Help me, angels!"

He hesitated and then said, "Let me make an effort with all my might! Bow, stubborn knees! Heart, which is held in place with strings of steel, be as soft as the sinews of a newborn babe!

"All may yet be well."

King Claudius knelt and attempted to pray.

Hamlet entered the room and saw King Claudius on his knees.

Hamlet said to himself, "Now I can easily kill the King, now while he is praying, and so I will do it."

He drew his sword and said to himself, "I will kill him, he will go to Heaven, and so I will have my revenge.

"Let me think about this. A villain murders my father, and in return for that murder, I, my father's sole son, send this same villain to Heaven.

"The villain should pay me to do that! Being sent to Heaven is a reward; sending someone to Heaven is not revenge.

"He murdered my father when my father was unprepared for death and for being judged. My father was full of bread; he was not fasting in penitence for his sins. My father died when all his sins were in full flower and as flush as May.

"Who knows this villain's spiritual account except Heaven? But according to our society and our way of thinking, he is heavy with sin.

"Would I be revenged if I were to kill him while he is purging his sin? He would be in a state of grace, and he would be prepared for death and for being judged. My father would suffer, while this villain enjoys Paradise.

"No. That would not be revenge. Sword, I will put you away."

He sheathed his sword, and then he said quietly, "Sword, a more horrid opportunity shall arise and I will use you then. I will use you when this villain is drunk and asleep, when he is furious, when he is enjoying incestuous pleasure in his bed, when he is gambling, when he is swearing, or when he is doing some act that has no taste of salvation in it. That is when I will trip him so that his heels will kick out at Heaven as he falls headfirst into Hell. When he dies, I want his soul to be as damned and black as Hell, to where it will go. I want his soul to be eternally damned.

"My mother is waiting for me.

"King Claudius, this physic, this medicine, merely prolongs your wretched life for a short while longer."

Hamlet exited.

King Claudius, who was unaware that Hamlet had been in the room, rose from his kneeling position and said to himself, "My words fly up, my thoughts remain below: Words without thoughts never to Heaven go. Words without true repentance are useless and meaningless. Unless there is true repentance, there is no forgiveness."

In the Queen's private chamber, Queen Gertrude and Polonius were talking.

Polonius said, "Hamlet will be here very soon. Speak frankly to him: Tell him his rude behavior has been too outrageous to bear with, and tell him that your grace has screened him from and stood between him and severe criticism.

"I will hide myself here behind this arras. I'll be quiet now. Please, be forthright when you speak to him."

Hamlet called from outside the room, "Mother, mother, mother!"

Queen Gertrude said to Polonius, "Don't worry about me. Hide. I can hear him coming."

Polonius hid behind the wall hanging.

Hamlet entered the room and asked, "Now, mother, what's the matter?"

"Hamlet, you have your father much offended."

She was referring to King Claudius.

"Mother, you have my father much offended."

He was referring to the late King Hamlet.

"Come, come, you answer me with an idle tongue."

"Go, go, you question me with a wicked tongue."

"Why, what are you saying, Hamlet!"

"What's the matter now?"

"Have you forgotten who I am?"

"No, by the cross on which Christ hung, I have not forgotten who you are. You are the Queen, you are your husband's brother's wife. And — I wish that it were not so! — you are my mother."

According to the Book of Common Prayer, "*A woman may not marry with her [...] Husband's Brother.*" Hamlet was accusing his mother of a forbidden marriage.

Queen Gertrude said, "I will not speak to you while you are like this. I will bring you some people to whom you can speak."

She stood up, but Hamlet forced her to sit back down.

He said, "Come, come, and sit yourself down. You shall not budge from here. You may not leave until I set up a mirror in front of you that will make you see the inmost part of yourself."

"What are you going to do?" Queen Gertrude asked. "Are you are going to murder me?"

She screamed, "Help! Help!"

Polonius screamed from behind the wall hanging, "Help! Help! Help!"

Hamlet drew his sword and said, "What is this! A rat? They get killed because they are always making noise and drawing attention to themselves. This rat is dead. I will bet a ducat that it will soon be dead; I will take a ducat for killing it."

He thrust his sword through the wall hanging and stabbed Polonius.

Polonius moaned, "I have been killed!"

He fell and died.

"What have you done!" Queen Gertrude said.

"I am not sure," Hamlet replied. "Is it the King?"

"What a rash and bloody deed this is!"

"A bloody deed!" Hamlet replied. "Almost as bad, good mother, as to kill a King, and marry his brother."

"As kill a King!" a shocked Queen Gertrude said.

"Yes, lady, that is what I said."

Hamlet was shocked that his mother had allowed someone to spy on what he thought was a private conversation with her. In his shock, he voiced his fear that his mother was complicit in Claudius' murder of King Hamlet, although the ghost had not told him that. Witnessing his mother's reaction to the accusation that she had helped kill her first husband, Hamlet became convinced that she was innocent of that sin.

Hamlet lifted the wall hanging and found Polonius.

He said to the corpse, "You wretched, rash, intruding fool, farewell! I mistook you for your better: I thought you were the King. Take your fortune. You have learned that to be too inquisitive is to put yourself in danger."

He said to his shocked mother, "Stop wringing your hands. Be quiet! Sit down, and let me wring your heart. I will do that if your heart can be penetrated by feeling — if damned habitual sins have not hardened your heart like brass so that no feeling can penetrate it."

"What have I done, that you dare wag your tongue so loudly and so rudely against me?"

"You have committed an act that blurs the grace and blush of modesty, calls virtue hypocritical, takes off the rose — female perfection — from the fair forehead of an innocent love and sets a blister — the branding of a prostitute — there, and makes marriage-vows as false as the oaths of people who gamble with dice," Hamlet replied. "You have committed a deed that plucks the soul out of and makes void marriage vows and turns sweet religion into a confused and meaningless pile of words. Heaven's hot face glows with shame above the Earth. Heaven is sorrowful, just as it will be on Judgment Day, because it is sickened by your act."

"Tell me," Queen Gertrude said, "what act have I committed that roars so loud, and thunders in these, your words that introduce your accusation of my act?"

On a necklace, Hamlet wore a miniature portrait of his father: the late King Hamlet. On a necklace, Queen Gertrude wore a miniature portrait of her husband: the present King Claudius.

Hamlet took the miniature portraits and held them side-by-side.

He said, "Look here, upon this picture, and upon this one. They are counterfeits — mere pictures — of two brothers.

"See, what a grace was seated on this brow — the brow of my late father. He is like the ancient mythological gods. He has the curled hair of Hyperion, the Sun-god. He has the forehead of Jove himself, King of gods and men. He has eyes like those of Mars, the god of war — eyes that threaten and command. He has a stance like that of the herald Mercury, messenger to the other gods, newly alighted on a hill so high that it kisses Heaven. My late father had a group of features and a form indeed, on which every god did seem to set his seal, to give the world assurance that this was a model man.

"That man was your first husband.

"But look now at the other portrait. Here is your second and present husband. He is like a moldy ear of corn, infecting his wholesome brother.

"Have you eyes?

"Could you leave this fair mountain — my father — to feed and gorge yourself on this barren moor? Ha! Do you have eyes?

"You cannot call it love because at your age the heyday in the blood — the passionate sexual period of life — is tame. It's humble, and it waits upon reason.

It obeys reason, and what reason would step from this, my father, to this, your second husband?

"Sense, surely, you have, or else you would not have the power of motion; but surely, that sense is paralyzed.

"Madness would never err in this way, and never has reason been so enthralled to sexual passion but that it was still able to make a choice between two such different alternatives.

"Your senses, madness, and reason could never choose King Claudius over the late King Hamlet.

"What devil was it then that thus has tricked you while you were playing Blind Man's Bluff?

"Eyes without feeling, feeling without sight, ears without hands or eyes, smelling without any of the other senses, or even just a sickly part of one true sense could not be so unaware as to choose King Claudius over the late King Hamlet.

"For shame! Where is your blush? Rebellious Hellish sexual desires, if you can mutiny in a matron's bones, then to flaming youth let virtue be like wax, and melt in her own fire. Proclaim no shame when the compulsive ardor of sexual desire gives the impetus to perform sexual misdeeds since frosty old age itself actively burns just like youthful sexual desire and since reason becomes a panderer for the passion. If old people are ruled by their sexual passion, what hope do young people have to resist such passion?"

"Oh, Hamlet, speak no more," Queen Gertrude said. "You made my eyes look deep into my soul, and there I see such black and engrained spots whose tincture — color — will not be washed away."

What sin is Queen Gertrude speaking about? She is not complicit in the murder of her first husband. Is she speaking only of her hasty second marriage or of something in addition to that? Adultery while her first husband was still alive, perhaps?

Hamlet replied, "No, it will not be washed away. And you are living in the rank sweat of a bed stained with the fluids of sex, stewed in corruption, honeying and making love over the nasty sty —"

Hamlet was punning again. The word "stewed" also referred to stewed prunes, which were served in brothels; as a result, "stews" became a slang word for brothels.

"Oh, speak to me no more," Queen Gertrude said. "These words of yours, like daggers, enter my ears. No more, sweet Hamlet!"

"King Claudius is a murderer and a villain; he is a slave who is not worth one-twentieth of a tithe — one-twentieth of ten percent — of your first husband. He is an unscrupulous monster among Kings; he is a cutpurse of the empire and the throne. From a shelf he stole the precious crown and put it in his pocket!"

The word "tithe" has religious significance because a Christian is supposed to tithe — give ten percent of income to charity and/or the church. In addition, the number "ten" has religious significance because ten is composed of three threes and one one. Three is the number of the Trinity, and one is the number of the Unity that is the Trinity. The Father, the Son, and the Holy Ghost become the one true God.

"No more!" Queen Gertrude pleaded.

"He is a King made of bits and pieces —"

The ghost entered the room.

Hamlet saw the ghost and prayed, "Save me, and hover over me with your wings, you Heavenly guards!"

He then said to the ghost, "What does your gracious figure want?"

Queen Gertrude could not see the ghost. To her, it seemed as if Hamlet were speaking to empty air.

She said, "Hamlet is mad! He is insane!"

Hamlet said to the ghost, "Have you come to reproach your tardy son, who, surprised by you in a time and while feeling the emotions that are important in fulfilling your dread command, is still not yet carrying out that command? Tell me!"

Hamlet was filled with emotion, but he was not doing what the ghost wanted him to do. The ghost wanted Hamlet to get revenge on King Claudius, and the ghost did not want Hamlet to hurt his mother. Hamlet had passed up an opportunity to kill King Claudius, and he was now emotionally hurting his mother.

The ghost said to Hamlet, "Do not forget what I told you. The purpose of this visitation is to whet your almost blunted purpose. But, look, your mother is bewildered. Step in between her and her soul as it fights frightening images. The imagination works strongest in the weakest bodies. Speak to her, Hamlet."

The ghost wanted Hamlet to take care of his mother and then to turn his attention to killing King Claudius.

"How are you, lady?" Hamlet asked his mother.

"How are *you*, Hamlet?" Queen Gertrude replied. "Why are you looking at nothing and speaking to empty air? Your eyes look wild as they wildly look, and your hair, like sleeping soldiers suddenly awakened by an alarm, is shocked and stands on end. Oh, gentle son, sprinkle cool patience upon the heat and flame of your distemper and illness. What are you looking at?"

"I am looking at him — at him!" Hamlet said as he pointed to the ghost. "Look, can't you see how pale he is as he stares! If his appearance and his reason for appearing here could conjoin together and preach to stones, they would make them responsive to his words."

He said to the ghost, "Do not look at me unless with piteous action you divert my stern deeds. If that happens, then what I have to do may lack the true color. Perhaps clear tears will flow instead of red blood."

When Hamlet first saw the ghost, the ghost had told Hamlet not to pity him. The ghost wanted violent action and blood instead of pity and tears.

"To whom are you speaking?" Queen Gertrude asked.

"Do you see nothing there?"

"I see nothing at all; yet I see everything that there is to see."

"Did you hear anything?"

"No, nothing but ourselves."

"Why, look there! Look at how it is moving away! It is my father, wearing the clothing he used to wear when he was alive! Look, he is leaving now — he is going out the door!"

The ghost exited.

"This is only the invention of your brain," Queen Gertrude said. "Madness is very cunning and skillful in creating things without bodies."

"Madness!" Hamlet said. "My pulse, just like yours, temperately keeps time, and makes as healthful music. What I have said is not the result of madness. Put me to the test, and I will repeat everything that I have said — that is an act that madness would run away from.

"Mother, for the love of Heaven, do not apply a soothing ointment to your soul by believing that it is my madness speaking and not your sin. The flattering ointment will only put a skin over the ulcerous place while rank corruption, undermining everything underneath the layer of skin, infects unseen.

"Confess your sins to Heaven. Repent what sins are past; avoid the temptations to come. And do not spread compost on the weeds to make them ranker.

"Forgive me this virtuous sermonizing of mine because in the fatness and grossness of these pursy — corpulent and purse-proud — times virtue itself must beg pardon from vice. Yes, virtue must bow and woo for permission to do vice good."

"Oh, Hamlet, you have broken my heart in two."

"Throw the worse part of your heart away, and live all the purer with the other half," Hamlet replied.

He added, "Good night, but do not go to my uncle's bed. If you do not really have a particular virtue, act as if you have it. The monster custom eats up all understanding of evil when we habitually do evil deeds, but it is angelic in this: When one practices fair and good actions, they become habitual. Doing evil deeds can become a habit, but so can doing good deeds. We can put on good or bad habits the way that we put on good or bad clothing. It is our choice.

"Refrain from having sex with King Claudius tonight, and that shall lend a kind of easiness to the next abstinence. The abstinence after that will be even easier. Habit can almost change the stamp of nature — our inborn characteristics.

"Habit can either welcome the Devil, or powerfully throw him out.

"Once more, good night. And when you are desirous to be blessed and ask for God's blessing, I'll beg a blessing from you like a dutiful son."

Hamlet pointed to the corpse of Polonius and said, "I repent killing this lord, but Heaven has been pleased to punish me with this corpse and to punish this corpse with me. It has been the will of Heaven that I be punished and that I punish Polonius. I have acted as Heaven's agent and minister of justice, and Heaven has punished me. I will dispose of him, and I will atone for the death I gave him.

"So, again, good night.

"I must be cruel only to be kind. Thus bad begins and worse remains behind. The death of Polonius is a bad beginning, and worse is still to come.

"One word more, good lady."

"What shall I do?" Queen Gertrude asked.

Hamlet said, "Here are things that I tell you NOT to do, no matter what happens:

"Let the bloated King tempt you again to go to bed. Let him pinch your cheek wantonly. Let him call you his mouse. Let him, because he gave you a few filthy kisses or stroked your neck with his damned fingers, convince you to disentangle everything for him."

She could disentangle her clothing and her hair dressing.

Hamlet continued with another thing NOT to tell Claudius: "Tell him that I am not mad essentially but am mad only in craft and cunning."

He said sarcastically, "It would be good for you to let him know that I am faking my madness because who would hide from a toad, from a bat, or from a tomcat such dear information concerning him? Who would do such a thing? A queen, fair, sober, and wise?"

With more sarcasm, he added, "No, to spite sense and secrecy, you ought to climb on top of a house with a basket of birds, open the basket and let the birds fly out. Then you ought to imitate the experimenting ape in the famous story and climb into the basket, jump out and try to fly like the birds, and break your neck when you fall to the ground."

"Be assured, Hamlet," Queen Gertrude said, "if words are made of breath, and breath is made of life, I have no life to breathe what you have said to me. I will not tell my husband what you have told me."

"I must go to England; do you know that?"

"Yes, I had forgotten, but it has been so decided."

"The letters are sealed, and my two schoolfellows, Rosencrantz and Guildenstern, whom I will trust as I trust fanged venomous snakes, bear the mandate — King Claudius' letter to the English King. They must sweep my way clear and carry me off and lead me into some trap.

"So be it. It will be fun to have the engineer be hoist with his own petard — blown up with his own bomb. Things shall go badly for me unless I can outwit the enemy and use the enemy's own bomb to blow him at the Moon. Oh, it is very sweet when two plots — the King's and mine — meet head-on.

"This man — the dead Polonius — shall cause me to be sent to England in a hurry and shall cause me to begin my plotting. I'll lug the guts into the neighboring room.

"Mother, good night.

"Indeed, this counselor is now very still, very secret, and very grave, although when he was alive he was a foolish prating knave."

Hamlet said to the corpse, "Come, sir, I will draw toward an end with you."

He added, "Good night, mother."

Hamlet then began to drag away the corpse of Polonius.

CHAPTER 4

— 4.1 —

In a room of the castle, King Claudius, Queen Gertrude, Rosencrantz, and Guildenstern were meeting.

"There's a reason for these sighs, these profound heaves," King Claudius said to Queen Gertrude, who was upset by her encounter with Hamlet. "You must translate them into language we can understand; it is fitting that we understand the reason for these sighs.

"Where is your son?"

Queen Gertrude said to Rosencrantz and Guildenstern, "Leave us alone here for a little while."

Rosencrantz and Guildenstern left the room.

"Ah, my good lord, what I have seen tonight!" Queen Gertrude said.

"What, Gertrude? How is Hamlet?"

"Hamlet is as mad as the sea and wind, when both contend in a storm to see which is the mightier. In his lawless and uncontrollable fit, Hamlet heard something stir behind the arras. He whipped out his rapier and cried, 'A rat, a rat!' Then, suffering from a delusion, he killed Polonius, the unseen good old man."

"What a heavy and grievous deed!" King Claudius said. "I would have been killed, if I had been there. Hamlet's liberty is full of threats to everyone: to you yourself, to us the King, to everyone.

"How shall this bloody deed be explained? Responsibility for it will be laid on us, whose providence should have kept this mad young man restrained and out of circulation, but we loved him so much that we would not understand what was the best course of action. Instead, I acted like someone suffering from a foul disease, who rather than let knowledge of it become public, let it remain uncured with the result that eventually it fed even on the essential substance of life.

"Where has Hamlet gone?"

"He is removing the body he has killed," Queen Gertrude said. "Even in his madness, he weeps over the corpse and feels remorse. This remorse is like some pure gold that shows itself in a mine of base metals."

"Gertrude, come away!" King Claudius said. "The Sun no sooner shall touch the mountains and bring the morning than we will ship Hamlet away from here. We must, with all our majesty and skill, both accept responsibility for and excuse Hamlet's vile deed."

He called, "Guildenstern!"

Rosencrantz and Guildenstern returned to the room.

King Claudius said to them, "Friends, go and get some men to assist you. Hamlet in his madness has slain Polonius, and he has dragged him away from his mother's private chamber.

"Go and find Hamlet. Speak politely and respectfully to him, and bring the body into the chapel. Please, hurry and do this."

Rosencrantz and Guildenstern left the room to carry out their orders.

King Claudius said, "Come, Gertrude, we'll call up our wisest friends, and we will let them know both what we mean to do and what has been unfortunately done. Oh, come away! My soul is full of discord and dismay."

— 4.2 —

In another room of the castle, Hamlet said to himself, "The corpse has been safely stowed away."

Rosencrantz and Guildenstern called, "Hamlet! Hamlet! Hamlet!"

"What noise is that?" Hamlet said. "Who is calling for me? Oh, here they come."

Rosencrantz and Guildenstern entered the room.

"What have you done, my lord, with the dead body?" Rosencrantz asked.

"I have mixed it with dust, to which it is kin," Hamlet said.

He was thinking of Genesis 3:19: "*In the sweat of thy face shalt thou eat bread, till thou return unto the ground; for out of it wast thou taken: for dust thou art, and unto dust shalt thou return.*"

Hamlet had not buried the corpse; he had simply placed it in a dusty room.

"Tell us where it is, so that we may take it from there and carry it to the chapel," Rosencrantz said.

"Do not believe it," Hamlet said.

"Believe what?" Rosencrantz asked.

"That I will do what you want me to do and not do what I want to do," Hamlet said. "When a sponge demands something, what reply should the son of a King make?"

"Do you think that I am a sponge, my lord?" Rosencrantz asked.

A sponge is a parasite who lives off other people. A sponge soaks up other people's money and other good things.

"Yes, sir, you are a sponge who soaks up the King's favor, his rewards, his powers. But such officers do the King best service in the end. He keeps them, like an ape does an apple, in the corner of his jaw. The ape first puts them in his mouth and then later swallows them. When the King needs what you have gleaned, he will squeeze you, and, you, sponge, shall be dry again."

Hamlet was warning Rosencrantz and Guildenstern that King Claudius was using them. Once King Claudius was done using them, Rosencrantz and Guildenstern would be discarded. Although Rosencrantz and Guildenstern were hoping for rewards from their master, serving a dangerous master would likely harm them.

97

"I do not understand you, my lord," Rosencrantz said.

"I am glad that you do not," Hamlet replied. "Fools are unable to understand irony."

"My lord, you must tell us where the body is, and go with us to the King," Rosencrantz said.

"The body is with the King, but the King is not with the body," Hamlet said.

Hamlet meant more than one thing here.

First, Polonius' physical body was with King Claudius because it was in the King's castle, but King Claudius was not with Polonius' body because Polonius' spiritual body was in Heaven.

Second, King Claudius' physical body was with him, but the body politic — what makes a King a true King — was not with him.

Hamlet added, "The King is a thing —"

Guildenstern exclaimed, "A thing, my lord!"

Hamlet continued, "— of nothing. Take me to him."

He then shouted, "Hide, fox, and all after!"

He ran off, and Rosencrantz and Guildenstern ran after him.

King Claudius said to some lords, "I have sent Rosencrantz and Guildenstern to seek Hamlet, and to find the body of Polonius. How dangerous it is that this man goes loose! Yet we must not put the strong arm of law on him. Hamlet is beloved by the unreasoning multitude of people. They use their eyes, not their reason and judgment, to decide whom to like. In such cases, they focus on the punishment given to the offender and not on the offense that the offender committed.

"To make everything go smoothly and evenly, my suddenly sending Hamlet away must seem like the result of careful deliberation.

"Desperate diseases require desperate cures, or they are not cured."

Rosencrantz entered the room. Guildenstern stayed with Hamlet, guarding him, outside.

"How are you?" King Claudius asked him. "What has happened?"

"Hamlet will not tell us where he stowed the corpse of Polonius."

"Where is Hamlet?"

"Outside, my lord. He is being guarded. What do you want done with him?"

"Bring him here before us," King Claudius said.

"Guildenstern!" Rosencrantz called. "Bring in my lord."

Hamlet and Guildenstern entered the room.

"Now, Hamlet, where's Polonius?" King Claudius asked.

"At supper."

"At supper! Where?"

"Do not ask where he eats, but where he is eaten," Hamlet said. "A certain convocation of politic — shrewd — worms is even now gnawing at him."

Hamlet was punning on the Diet of Worms, which was held in the German city of Worms in 1521. The word "diet" means "council." Holy Roman Emperor Charles V presided over the Diet of Worms.

Hamlet continued, "Your worm is your only Emperor for diet. We fatten all other creatures so that we can eat them and grow fat ourselves, and we ourselves grow fat so that we can feed maggots. A fat King and a lean beggar are only two different courses at a meal; they are two dishes on one table. That's the end for us."

"Alas! Alas!" King Claudius said.

"A man may fish with a worm that has eaten part of a King, and then he can eat the fish that has fed on that worm."

"What do you mean by this?"

"Nothing except to show you how a King may progress through the guts of a beggar," Hamlet replied.

"Where is Polonius?"

"In Heaven; send someone there to see," Hamlet replied. "If your messenger does not find him there, then seek him in the other place yourself. But indeed, if you do not find him within this month, you shall smell him as you go up the stairs into the lobby."

King Claudius said to some attendants, "Go seek the corpse there."

"He will stay until you come," Hamlet said to the attendants as they were leaving the room.

"Hamlet, because of this deed, for your own personal safety — which we dearly care for, just as we dearly grieve for this deed that you have done — we must send you away from here with fiery quickness. Therefore prepare yourself to travel. The ship is ready, and the wind is blowing in the right direction, your companions are waiting for you, and everything is ready for you to go to England."

"For England?"

"Yes, Hamlet."

"Good."

"So it is, as you would know if you knew our motives."

"I see a cherub who sees them," Hamlet replied.

He suspected King Claudius' motives, and he was reminding King Claudius that God and the angels in Heaven know everything.

Hamlet continued, "Let's go to England!"

He said to King Claudius, "Farewell, dear mother."

King Claudius replied, "Your loving father, Hamlet."

"You are my mother. Father and mother are man and wife; man and wife are one flesh; and so, you are my mother.

"Let's go to England!"

Hamlet exited.

King Claudius ordered Rosencrantz and Guildenstern, "Follow him closely; persuade him to board the ship quickly. Do not delay. I'll have him leave here tonight. Away! Everything else needed for this journey to happen has been sealed and done. Please, hurry."

Rosencrantz and Guildenstern left the room.

King Claudius motioned with his hands, and everyone departed, leaving him alone.

King Claudius had written a letter to the King of England, a letter that Rosencrantz and Guildenstern would carry on board ship. Now he held an imaginary one-sided conversation with the English King:

"King of England, if you value at all my friendship — as you should, because of my great power ... your country can still feel the raw and red scar that it received from the Danish sword, and you are paying homage and tribute to us to keep our soldiers away — because of this, you cannot coldly set aside and ignore our royal command, which is described in full in a letter: the immediate death of Hamlet. Do it, King of England — kill Hamlet.

"Hamlet rages like a fever in my blood, and you must cure me. Until I know that Hamlet is dead, whatever else happens, I will never be happy."

On a plain in Denmark, young Fortinbras, one of his Captains, and an army of soldiers were marching.

Fortinbras ordered, "Go, Captain, and give the Danish King my greetings. Tell him that, in accordance with our agreement, Fortinbras craves safe conduct and an escort as he marches across Denmark. You know the rendezvous. If his majesty wants to see us, we will pay his respects to him in person. Tell him that."

"I will do so, my lord," the Captain replied.

Fortinbras ordered his army, "March onward. Do nothing to cause trouble."

Fortinbras and his army marched onward, leaving the Captain behind.

Hamlet, Rosencrantz, Guildenstern, and others arrived.

Hamlet said to the Captain, "Good sir, whose soldiers are these?"

"They are Norwegian, sir," the Captain replied.

"Please tell me where they are marching, sir."

"They are marching to fight in a part of Poland."

"Who commands them, sir?"

"Fortinbras, the nephew to the aged King of Norway."

"Will his army fight the heartland of Poland, or will it fight some frontier?"

"To speak truly, and with no exaggeration, we go to fight to gain a little patch of ground that has in it no profit but the name. Whoever wins the battle will gain nothing but reputation — he will win the name of conqueror. I would not rent it for five — five! — ducats. It would not bring in more to either the King of Norway or the King of Poland if it were sold outright. It is a worthless piece of land."

"Why, then the King of Poland will never defend it."

"Yes, he will," the Captain said. "He has already stationed soldiers there."

"Two thousand souls and twenty thousand ducats will not settle this straw — this trivial matter," Hamlet said. "This is the abscess that results from having too much wealth during peacetime. The abscess festers inside the body and the man dies without other people knowing why.

"I humbly thank you, sir."

The Captain replied, "May God be with you, sir," and departed.

Rosencrantz asked Hamlet, "Will it please you to go, my lord?"

"I'll be with you very quickly. Go ahead of me a little distance," Hamlet replied.

Everyone started traveling again, leaving Hamlet alone.

Hamlet said to himself, "Everything denounces me and spurs me on to get my delayed revenge! What is a man, if his chief happiness and all he does with his time is simply to sleep and eat? He is a beast — no more than that. Surely, He Who made us with such a fine power of reasoning, which we can use to learn from the past and plan for the future, did not give us that capability and God-like reason to go unused by us and get moldy. Now, whether it be due to an animal's forgetfulness or from some cowardice caused by thinking in too much detail on the outcome of our action — a thought that, divided into four parts, has but one part wisdom and three parts cowardice — I do not know why I yet live to say, 'This thing is something I have to do.' It should have been done already. After all, I have the reason — a cause — and the will and the strength and the means to do it.

"Examples as weighty as Earth exhort me to take action and get revenge. Witness this army of such size and expense that is being led by a delicate and tender Prince with a spirit that is puffed up with divine ambition and who makes a face at and scorns the unknown outcome of his war. He is exposing what is mortal and unsure to all that fortune, death, and danger dare. And for what? For an eggshell.

"Rightly to be great is not to stir without great argument, but greatly to find quarrel in a straw when honor is at stake."

Hamlet thought, *It is true that the way to get a reputation is not by refraining from making war unless you have a good reason for making war, but by making war over a trifle — a straw — when honor is at stake.*

If Fortinbras had said that this trifle of land in Poland is not worth fighting for and so I will remain at home instead of going to war, he would gain no reputation. But since he is willing to go to war and get lots of soldiers killed and lots of money spent over a trifle, he will gain a reputation. But will it be a negative or a positive reputation?

Or perhaps the right way to be great is to not make war unless you have an excellent reason for making war, but people mistakenly think that the right way to be great is to make war over a trifle — a straw — when honor is at stake. But will it be negative or positive greatness?

Hamlet said, "But what about me? I am not concerned with trifles and straws. I have a father who has been murdered, a mother whose character has been stained, and incentives both in my mind and in my emotions to take action and get revenge, and what have I done? I have slept and done nothing. Meanwhile, to my shame, I see the imminent death of twenty thousand men, who, merely for Fortinbras' fantasy and illusion of fame, go to their graves as if the graves were beds. They will die while fighting for a plot of land that is not big enough to contain all the soldiers fighting over it and which is not big enough to provide tombs and graves for all the soldiers who will die fighting over it.

"Oh, from this time forth, my thoughts will be bloody, or they will be worth nothing!"

— 4.5 —

In a room in the castle at Elsinore, Queen Gertrude was talking with Horatio and a gentleman about Ophelia.

"I will not speak with her," Queen Gertrude said.

"She is insistent, indeed distraught," the gentleman said. "Her state of mind ought to be pitied."

"What does she want?"

"She speaks a lot about her father; she says that she hears there's tricks in the world; and she makes sounds, and she beats her heart," the gentleman said. "She takes offense at trifles and straws, and she speaks ambiguously and says things that are only half-sensible. Her speech is nonsense, but because it is nonsense her hearers attempt to make sense of it. They work hard at understanding it, and they interpret her words to fit what they think. Her winks, and her nods, and her gestures convince them that her words must have meaning. Although they are not sure what that meaning is, they think that it must be an unhappy meaning."

Horatio advised Queen Gertrude, "It is a good idea to talk to her because she may cause ill-breeding minds to make dangerous conjectures."

"Let her come in," Queen Gertrude said.

The gentleman left to tell Ophelia to come into the room.

Queen Gertrude thought, *To my sick soul — sin's true nature is sickness — each trifle seems to be the prologue to some great misfortune. So full of artless jealousy is guilt, it spills itself in fearing to be spilt. Guilt is so full of uncontrolled suspicion that it reveals itself because it so much fears to be revealed. The guilty act guilty because they are so afraid of being found out to be guilty.*

Ophelia entered the room.

"Where is the beauteous majesty of Denmark?" Ophelia asked.

"How are you, Ophelia?"

Ophelia sang, "*How should I your true love know*

"*From another one?*

"*By his cockle hat and staff,*

"*And his sandal shoon.*"

Ophelia was singing about a lover who was dressed like a pilgrim. In his hat he wore a "cockle," aka scallop shell, he carried a staff, and he wore sandals for his shoes. A pilgrim was someone who was going or had gone on a pilgrimage or journey to a religious site. Pilgrims who were returning from a pilgrimage to the shrine of St. James in Compostela, Spain, wore a cockle shell in their hat. Lovers sometimes disguised themselves as religious pilgrims to get access to those whom they loved.

"Alas, sweet lady, what is the meaning of this song?" Queen Gertrude asked.

"What did you say?" Ophelia asked. "Please, listen."

She sang, "*He is dead and gone, lady,*

"*He is dead and gone;*

"*At his head a grass-green plot,*

"*At his heels a tombstone.*"

"But, Ophelia —" Queen Gertrude started to say.

"Please, listen," Ophelia replied.

She sang, "*White his shroud as the mountain snow —*"

King Claudius entered the room.

Queen Gertrude said to him, "Alas, look here, my lord."

Ophelia sang, "*Sprinkled all over with sweet flowers*

"*Which bewept to the grave did go*

"*With true-love showers.*"

"How are you, pretty lady?" King Claudius asked.

"May God reward you," Ophelia replied. "They say the owl was a baker's daughter. Lord, we know what we are, but we do not know what we may become. May God be at your table!"

According to an old legend, Christ, who appeared to be a beggar, asked a baker for food. The baker was a charitable person who put a large piece of dough in an oven to bake, but his daughter criticized him for putting such a large piece of dough in the oven — she wanted the beggar to be given less food. Because the baker's daughter was not charitable, she was turned into an owl.

"She is distressed about her father," King Claudius said.

"Please, let's have no words about this," Ophelia said, "but when they ask you what it means, say this."

She sang, "*Tomorrow is Saint Valentine's Day,*

"*All in the morning early,*

"And I a maiden at your window,

"To be your Valentine.

"Then up he rose, and donned his clothes,

"And opened up the chamber-door;

"Let in the maiden, that out a maiden

"Never departed more."

According to a folk belief, the first young person of the opposite sex that young men and young women would see on Saint Valentine's Day would be their one true love.

"Pretty Ophelia!" King Claudius said.

"Indeed, la, without an oath," she said, "I'll make an end of it."

She sang, *"By Gis and by Saint Charity,*

"Alack, and fie for shame!

"Young men will do it, if they come to it;

"By Cock, they are to blame.

"Quoth she, 'Before you tumbled me,

"'You promised me to wed.'

"He answers,

"'So would I have done, by yonder Sun,

"'If you had not come to my bed.'"

"Gis" meant "Jesus." "Do it" meant "to have sex." "Cock" meant "God" — and an obvious additional meaning. "Tumbled me" meant "to have sex with me"; in this context, it included the meaning of "took my virginity."

"How long has she been like this?" King Claudius asked.

"I hope all will be well," Ophelia said. "We must be patient, but I cannot choose but weep, to think they should lay him in the cold ground. My brother shall know about it, and so I thank you for your good counsel. Come, my coach! Good night, ladies; good night, sweet ladies; good night, good night."

Ophelia exited from the room.

"Follow her closely; watch her closely, please," King Claudius said to Horatio.

Horatio followed Ophelia, leaving the King and Queen alone.

"Oh, this is the poison of deep grief," King Claudius said about Ophelia's insanity. "It springs entirely from her father's death. Oh, Gertrude, Gertrude, when sorrows come, they come not singly like spies sent separately ahead to scout the land, but in whole battalions. First, her father was slain. Next, Hamlet, your son, has gone, and he was the most violent author of his own just exile. The people are confused; their thoughts and whispers are muddied and troubled and unhealthy and suspicious about the death of good Polonius. We have acted foolishly by hurrying to secretly inter him. Poor Ophelia is insane, divorced from her rational judgment, without which we are pictures —mere images of human beings — or mere beasts. Finally, and just as serious as all of these other ills, Ophelia's brother — Laertes — has in secret returned to Denmark from France. He broods over his bewilderment, he does not seek the truth but remains ignorant of it. He has gossip-mongers buzzing in his ears and telling him pestilential stories about his father's death. Because Laertes does not know the truth, he must of necessity believe me to be guilty because he must blame someone. This is a supposition that he will tell others. Oh, my dear Gertrude, this multitude of troubles is killing me over and over just like a cannon fires and kills many soldiers with grapeshot — many small pieces of metal that are fired all at once and that scatter and kill."

They heard a noise in the castle.

"What is that noise?" Queen Gertrude asked. She was alarmed.

"Where are my Swiss guards?" King Claudius asked. "Let them guard the door!"

A messenger entered the room.

"What is the matter?" King Claudius asked.

"Save yourself, my lord," the messenger said. "The ocean, rising above its limits, does not overwhelm the flat, low-lying coastal lands with more impetuous haste than young Laertes, advancing with an army of rebels, overwhelms your military officers. The rabble call him lord, and, as if the world were now going to begin again, with all traditions and established customs that ratify and prop up civilization having been forgotten, they cry, 'We choose Laertes to be King.' They throw their hats into the air, they applaud with their hands, and their tongues cry to the clouds, 'Laertes shall be King! Laertes shall be King!'"

"How cheerfully they cry like hounds as they follow a false trail!" Queen Gertrude said. "These false Danish hounds are tracking counter — they are following the scent the wrong way! They trace the trail backwards!"

Laertes was looking for the person who had killed his father, but Hamlet's trail led away from Elsinore and toward England. Laertes and his followers were heading toward Elsinore.

They heard noises, and King Claudius said, "The doors have been broken."

Laertes and a number of his armed followers rushed into the room.

"Where is this King?" Laertes asked, contemptuously.

He said to his armed followers, "Sirs, all of you stand outside the room."

His followers protested, "No, let us come in."

Laertes replied, "Please, if you don't mind."

"We will obey," his armed followers said.

As they left the room, Laertes said to them, "I thank you. Guard the door."

He then said to King Claudius, "Oh, you vile King, give me my father!"

"Be calm, good Laertes," Queen Gertrude said, holding on to him.

"Any drop of my blood that is calm proclaims me to be a bastard," Laertes replied. "Any drop of my blood that is calm cries that my father is a cuckold and that my mother is a harlot with the brand of a whore on her forehead. If I am truly my father's son, and if my mother has been faithful to her husband, then every drop of my blood is outraged by his death."

"What is the reason, Laertes, that your rebellion looks so giant-like?" King Claudius asked. "This rebellion is like that of the giants Otus and Ephialtes, who tried to make war on the Olympian gods.

"Let him go, Gertrude. Do not fear for our person. Such divinity protects a King that treason can only peep at what it would like to do; it can act but little of what it wants to do."

And yet Claudius had succeeded in murdering his brother, King Hamlet.

King Claudius continued, "Tell me, Laertes, why you are so incensed and angry? Let him go, Gertrude."

She let go of Laertes.

"Speak, man," King Claudius said.

"Where is my father?" Laertes asked.

"Dead."

"But your father was not killed by the King," Queen Gertrude said.

"Let him ask whatever he wants to ask," King Claudius said to her.

"What is the cause of his death?" Laertes asked. "I'll not be trifled with and misled. To Hell with loyalty and allegiance! I will make vows to the blackest

Devil! I will damn my conscience and grace to the profoundest pit! I dare to be damned for all eternity on Judgment Day. I am resolved; I do not care about this world or the next. Let come what will come, but I will be revenged most thoroughly for the murder of my father."

"Who shall prevent you?" King Claudius asked.

"I swear that not all the world can stop me," Laertes replied. "And as for my resources, I'll manage them so well that although limited, they will go a long way."

"Good Laertes, if you desire to know with certainty the cause of your dear father's death, are you determined that in your revenge, like a gambler sweeping up all the money — including that belonging to winners as well as to losers — on a table, you will punish both friends and foes?"

"I will punish none but my father's enemies," Laertes replied.

"Would you like to know who are his friends and who are his enemies?"

"To my father's friends, I will open wide my arms, and like the kind life-rendering pelican, I will feed them with my blood — I am willing to die for them."

According to a folk tradition, the pelican fed its young with its own blood.

"Why, now you are speaking like a good child and a true gentleman," King Claudius said. "I will prove to you that I am guiltless of your father's death and that I grieve most sincerely for it. I will show my innocence to you as clearly as your eyes see daylight."

Laertes' men outside the door shouted, "Let her come in!"

Laertes said, "What's going on? What noise is that?"

Ophelia entered the room.

Immediately recognizing that Ophelia was insane, Laertes said, "Oh, heat, dry up and ruin my brains! Excessively salty tears, burn out the ability of my eyes to see! I would rather lose both my mind and my sight than to see Ophelia like this!

"By Heaven, Ophelia's madness shall be avenged! I will put my revenge into one side of a set of scales until it outweighs the harm done to you! Oh, rose of May! Dear maiden, kind sister, sweet Ophelia! Oh, Heavens! Is it possible that a young maiden's wits should be as mortal as an old man's life?

"Nature is exquisite in love, and when love is exquisite, it sends some precious part of itself after the thing it loves."

Laertes believed that Ophelia had gone mad because of the death of their father and that she had sent her sanity to join his spirit. This is a poetic way of saying that Ophelia's grief over the death of her father had driven her insane.

Ophelia sang, "*They bore him barefaced on the bier;*

"*Hey non nonny, nonny, hey nonny;*

"*And in his grave rained many a tear —*

"*Fare you well, my dove!*"

"If you had your wits and urged me to get revenge for the death of our father, you could not speak more persuasively," Laertes said.

Ophelia said to the King and Queen, "You must sing, '*A-down a-down.*'"

Then she said to her brother, Laertes, "And you must sing, '*A-down-a.*'"

These words were the refrain to her song.

Ophelia then said, "Oh, how the wheel — the refrain — becomes it! It is the false steward, who stole his master's daughter."

Ophelia's thoughts and songs were about the death of a loved one and about betrayal by a lover or "lover."

"This nonsense has more meaning in it than sensible speech has," Laertes said.

Ophelia said about the imaginary flowers she was "holding," "There's rosemary; that is for remembrance. Please, love, remember. And here are pansies; that is for thoughts."

She "presented" the imaginary flowers signifying remembrance to Laertes.

"Here is a lesson in madness," Laertes said. "She has fittingly linked thoughts and remembrance."

Ophelia said, "There's fennel for you, and columbines."

She "presented" the imaginary flowers signifying deceit (fennel) and marital infidelity (columbine) to Queen Gertrude.

Ophelia said, "There's rue for you."

She "presented" the imaginary rue — an herb — signifying sorrow and repentance to King Claudius.

Ophelia said, "And here's some rue for me. We may call rue 'herb-grace of Sundays.' Oh, you must wear your rue for a different reason. There's a daisy.

"I would give you some violets, but they all withered when my father died. They say that he made a good end —"

She sang, "*For bonny sweet Robin is all my joy.*"

The themes of Bonny Robin songs include lovers and unfaithfulness.

"She turns sadness and affliction, suffering, and Hell itself to charm and to prettiness," Laertes said.

Ophelia sang, "*And will he not come again?*

"*And will he not come again?*

"*No, no, he is dead:*

"*Go to your deathbed:*

"*He never will come again.*

"*His beard was as white as snow,*

"*All flaxen was his head:*

"*He is gone, he is gone,*

"*And we cast away moan:*

"*God have mercy on his soul!*"

She added, "And may God have mercy on all Christian souls, I pray. May God be with you."

She exited from the room.

"Do you see this, God?" Laertes prayed.

"Laertes, I must share in your grief, or you deny me something that is my right," King Claudius said. "Go and talk to your wisest friends. Let them judge the issue between you and me. If they find that I am implicated — whether directly or indirectly — in the death of your father, I will give you my Kingdom, my crown, my life, and all that I call mine, in recompense. But if they find me innocent, then be patient and let us work together to give your soul what it most wants: revenge."

"Let this be so," Laertes replied. "My father's means of death and his obscure funeral — he had no trophy, sword, or painting of his coat of arms over his bones, and he had no noble rite or formal ostentation — all cry out, as if my father's soul were shouting from Heaven to Earth, and so I demand an explanation of them."

"And so you shall receive an explanation," King Claudius said. "And where the offence is, let the great axe fall. Please, come with me."

They departed together.

In another room in the castle, Horatio said to a servant, "Who are they who would speak with me?"

"Sailors, sir," the servant replied. "They say they have letters for you."

"Let them come in."

The servant left to get the sailors.

Horatio said to himself, "I do not know from what part of the world I should be greeted, if not from Lord Hamlet."

Some sailors entered the room.

The first sailor said, "God bless you, sir."

"Let Him bless you, too," Horatio replied.

"He shall, sir, if it pleases Him," the first sailor said.

He handed Horatio a letter and said, "There's a letter for you, sir; it comes from the ambassador who was bound for England. This letter is for you, assuming that your name is Horatio, as I am told it is."

The letter was from Hamlet, who had told the sailors that he was an ambassador instead of telling them that he was a Prince and presumably the next in line to be King.

Horatio read the letter out loud.

"*Horatio, when you shall have looked over this letter, give these fellows some way to have contact with the King: They have letters for him. Before we were two days out at sea, a pirate ship ready to do battle chased us. Finding ourselves too slow of sail, we were forced to be brave and fight, and the pirates threw grappling irons to our ship. I crossed the lines to the pirate ship, and then the pirate ship and our ship separated with the result that I became the pirates' only prisoner. They have dealt with me like thieves of mercy — like merciful thieves — but they knew what they were doing. In return for their mercy, I am to do a good turn for them.*

"*Let the King have the letters I have sent and then come to me with as much speed as you would use to flee from death. I have words to speak in your ear that will make you speechless; yet they are much too light for the seriousness of the matter. These good fellows will bring you to where I am.*

"*Rosencrantz and Guildenstern still hold their course for England. Of them I have much to tell you.*

"*He whom you know to be your friend,*
"*HAMLET.*"

Horatio said to the sailors, "Come, I will give you help to deliver these letters of yours, and I will do that as quickly as possible so that you may take me to the man whose letters you brought."

In another room of the castle, King Claudius and Laertes were talking together, alone.

King Claudius said, "Now you must agree that I am not guilty of the death of your father, and you must regard me as a friend since you have heard and learned that the man who has slain your noble father has tried to kill me."

"It looks that way," Laertes replied. "But tell me why you did not try to punish the man who committed these deeds that are so criminal and punishable by death. Regard for your own safety, as well as wisdom and everything else, ought to have provoked you and made you punish him."

"I had two special reasons," King Claudius said. "To you they may seem very weak, but to me they are strong.

"The first reason is that the Queen his mother dotes on him. As for me — my virtue or my plague, whichever it is — she is such a part of my life and soul that, just like a star moves only in its orbit-sphere, I must be with her and move with her.

"My other reason, explaining why I could not try him in a public court, is that the general public loves him. They dip his faults in their affection, and they are like a spring that turns wood to stone by petrifying it; they convert his metaphorical fetters — his faults — to graces. And so my arrows, which are too slight to be used in such a wind, would have returned again to my bow — they would not have hit the target I aimed at."

"And so I have lost a noble father, and my sister has been driven into a desperate condition," Laertes said. "Her worth, if praises may go back again to what she used to be, offered a conspicuous challenge — as if she stood on a mountain — to others to equal her perfections. But my revenge will come."

"Don't toss and turn at night because of thinking about revenge," King Claudius said. "Don't think that I am made of stuff so flat and dull that I will let my beard be shook with danger and think that it is a joke and a game. You shortly shall hear more."

By sending Hamlet to England, King Claudius was hoping that Hamlet would soon be killed. King Claudius thought that he could soon tell Laertes that the man who had killed his father was dead.

King Claudius continued, "I loved your father, and I love myself, and that, I hope, will teach you to imagine "

A messenger entered the room, and King Claudius broke off what he was saying to Laertes and instead asked the messenger, "What is it? What is the news?"

"I bring letters, my lord, from Hamlet. This letter is to your majesty; this letter is to the Queen."

"From Hamlet! Who brought them?"

"Sailors, my lord, they say," the messenger replied. "I did not see them. These letters were given me by Claudio; he received them from the person who brought them."

King Claudius said, "Laertes, you shall hear this letter."

He ordered the messenger, "Leave us."

The messenger exited.

King Claudius read out loud the letter that Hamlet had written to him:

"High and mighty one,

"You need to know that I have been set naked — without any possessions — on the land of your Kingdom. Tomorrow I shall beg for permission to see your Kingly eyes. At that time, I shall, after first asking your pardon to do so, recount the occasion of my sudden and very strange return to Denmark.

"HAMLET."

King Claudius asked, "What does this mean? Have all the rest come back to Denmark, too? Or is this some trick, and Hamlet has not returned?"

"Do you know the handwriting?"

"It is Hamlet's handwriting," King Claudius said. "He writes, 'Naked'! And in a postscript here, he writes that he is 'alone.' Do you know anything about this?"

"I know nothing about it, my lord," Laertes replied. "But let Hamlet come. It warms the very sickness in my heart to know that I shall live and tell him to his teeth, 'You did this: You killed my father. And now you die.'"

"If the contents of this letter are true, Laertes — as how could they be otherwise? — will you allow yourself to be ruled by me? Will you do what I tell you to do?"

"Yes, my lord," Laertes said, "as long as you do not overrule my desires and order me to make peace with Hamlet."

"I want you to be at peace with yourself," King Claudius said. "If Hamlet has now returned to Denmark, rejecting his voyage to England and with no intention of undertaking it in the future, I will persuade him to undertake an exploit that will result in his death, and no one shall suspect ill play. Even his mother will think that Hamlet died by accident."

"My lord, I will do what you tell me to do," Laertes said. "I will especially do it if you can arrange for me to be the cause of Hamlet's death."

"I have an idea," King Claudius said. "You have been much talked about since your travels, and Hamlet has heard what people have said about you. They praise a skill in which you shine. None of your other good points made Hamlet as envious as that one skill, although in my opinion, that skill is not the best of those things in which you excel."

"What skill is that, my lord?" Laertes asked.

"It is a mere ribbon in the cap of youth," King Claudius said, "and yet it is a necessary skill, too. Light and careless clothing is as becoming to young people as is dark and serious clothing that denotes well being and seriousness to the old. Some things are suitable for young men, and other things are suitable for old men.

"Two months ago, a gentleman of Normandy visited here. I've seen and served against the French, and they can ride well on horseback, but this gallant Norman's skill on horseback had witchcraft in it. He seemed to grow into his seat, and he made his horse do such wondrous things that it was if he and his horse were one being, like a Centaur. He performed better than I ever imagined that a man could perform on horseback. Whatever I was able to conceive in my imagination, he outperformed."

"He was a Norman?"

"Yes, a Norman."

"I bet my life that his name was Lamond."

"The very same."

"I know him well," Laertes said. "He is the ornament and jewel indeed of all his nation."

"He said that he knew you, and he praised highly your skill in the exercise of the defensive arts. He especially praised your skill with the rapier. He cried out that it would indeed be a sight if anyone could match you. The fencers of France, he swore, would lack motion, guard, and eye, if you opposed them.

"Sir, Lamond's report about you inflamed Hamlet with such envy that he could do nothing but wish and beg that you would return to Denmark so that he could fence with you.

"Now, out of this ..." King Claudius started to say, and then he hesitated.

"What can come out of this, my lord?" Laertes asked.

"Laertes, was your father dear to you?" King Claudius asked. "Or are you like the painting of a sorrow — a mere face without a heart?"

"Why are you asking me this?"

"It is not the case that I think you did not love your father," King Claudius said. "But I know that time causes love to come into being, and I see from well-attested examples that time diminishes the spark and fire of love. There lives within the very flame of love a kind of wick that will burn and diminish and so will abate and lessen love. Love burns out; nothing remains the same. Even goodness, growing to excess, can die from that excess. Love can die slowly over time, and love can burn out through over-intensity.

"When should we do those things we ought to do? We should do them when we ought to do them. What we want and ought to do is subjected to weakenings and delays; there are as many weakenings and delays as there are tongues, and hands, and impediments.

"We have an awareness of what we ought to do and what we should do. Unless we take action and do those things, we are hurting ourselves. Taking the easy way out by not taking action may seem to be a kind of relief, but that is only appearance, not reality.

"But, to go to the quick — the most sensitive and painful part — of the ulcer, Hamlet is coming back to Elsinore.

"What are you willing to do that will show yourself to be your father's son in deed and not just in words?"

"I am willing to cut Hamlet's throat in the church," Laertes replied.

"No place, indeed, should be a sanctuary for a murderer," King Claudius said.

He meant that no place should be a sanctuary for Hamlet, but if Laertes were to murder Hamlet, then King Claudius' sentence would apply also to Laertes.

King Claudius continued, "Revenge should have no bounds."

He meant that Laertes' revenge should have no bounds, but his sentence could apply also to Hamlet's revenge.

King Claudius continued, "But, good Laertes, will you do what I want you to do? Will you stay hidden within your chamber? When Hamlet returns, he will learn that you are here. I will have other people praise your excellence in fencing; their praise will be added to that of the Norman.

"We will then finally bring you two together, and place bets on the duel. Hamlet is carelessly trusting; he is very magnanimous and he does not engage in deceitful practices, and so he will not closely inspect the swords. Therefore, you can easily — or, if need be, use some trickery to — choose a sword that has not been blunted. In the duel, you will kill him and avenge your father."

"I will do it," Laertes said. "And, to make sure I kill Hamlet, I'll anoint my sword with poison. I bought an ointment from a mountebank — a travelling quack. The ointment is so poisonous and deadly that if a knife that has been dipped in it draws blood, there is no mixture of medicines so strong that it can save the person who has been scratched.

"I will touch the point of my sword with this contagion, with the result that, if I touch him even slightly, he will die."

"Let me think further about this," King Claudius said. "Let me figure out which time and which method are most likely to work. If this plot should fail, and if our part in it should become known, it would have been better for us not to have tried it. Therefore, we should have a backup plan to kill Hamlet, in case this plan fails to work.

"Think! Let me see. We'll make a solemn wager on your respective skills — I have it!

"When in your duel you both are hot and dry — make the duel very active to achieve that end — and so Hamlet calls for something to drink, I'll have prepared a chalice of poisoned drink for him for the occasion. If Hamlet merely sips from the chalice, he will die, even if he escapes being injured by your poisoned sword."

Queen Gertrude entered the room.

King Claudius asked, "How are you, sweet Queen?"

"One woe treads upon another woe's heel, so fast they follow," she replied. "Ophelia, your sister, has drowned, Laertes."

"Drowned! Where?"

"There is a willow that is growing slantingly over a brook," Queen Gertrude replied. "The grey undersides of its leaves are reflected in the glassy waters of the stream. There Ophelia came with fantastic garlands of crow-flowers, non-stinging nettles, daisies, and long purple flowers that rudely speaking shepherds give a crude name, but that our chaste maidens call dead men's fingers.

"There, as she clambered on the boughs to hang her coronet weeds, an envious branch broke, and she and her flowery trophies fell in the weeping brook. Her clothes spread wide, and for a while they bore her up like a mermaid, during which time she chanted snatches of old tunes, like one who is incapable of understanding the danger she was in, or like a creature born and equipped to live in water, but before long her clothing, heavy with their drink, pulled the poor wretch from her melodious lay down to muddy death."

"Alas, then, she is drowned!" Laertes exclaimed.

"Drowned! Drowned!" Queen Gertrude said.

"Too much water you have had, poor Ophelia," Laertes said, "and therefore I forbid my tears to fall, but yet crying with grief is our way; nature must have her custom, let shame say what it will. When these tears are gone, the womanish part of me will be out of my body."

He said to King Claudius, "*Adieu*, my lord. I have a speech of fire, which would like to blaze, except that this folly of tears puts it out."

He exited from the room.

King Claudius said, "Let's follow him, Gertrude. How much effort I had to make to calm Laertes' rage! Now I fear this will start it up again. Therefore let's follow him."

CHAPTER 5

— 5.1 —

In a churchyard, two people — a gravedigger and his friend — talked about Ophelia's death.

"Is she to be buried in Christian ground although she willfully sought her own salvation?" the gravedigger asked.

People who were known to have committed suicide were not given Christian burials; they were not buried on consecrated ground such as that of the churchyard.

The gravedigger had said that Ophelia had sought her own salvation, but perhaps he meant that she had sought her own damnation since suicide was thought to be a violation of the commandment *"Thou shalt not kill"* (Exodus 20:13, King James Version). Or perhaps he meant her own destruction.

"I tell you she is," the friend said, "and therefore make her grave without delay. The coroner has sat on her, and he has ruled that she will get a Christian burial. He has ruled that she is not guilty of committing suicide."

By "sat on her," the friend meant "has held an inquest on her."

"How can that be, unless she drowned herself in her own defense?"

"Why, the coroner has made the decision."

"It must be *se offendendo*; it cannot be anything else," the gravedigger said.

Se offendendo means "self-offense," but perhaps the gravedigger meant *se defendendo*, which means "self-defense."

The gravedigger continued, "For here lies the point: If I drown myself wittingly, it argues an act, and an act has three branches. They are to act, to do, and to perform. *Argal*, she drowned herself wittingly."

By *Argal*, the gravedigger meant *Ergo*, which is Latin for "therefore."

"But listen, Mr. Gravedigger —"

"Allow me to explain. Here lies the water. Good. Here stands the man. Good. If the man goes to this water, and drowns himself, it is, whatever he may think about it, the end of him — note that.

"But if the water comes to him and drowns him, he does not drown himself; *argal*, he who is not guilty of his own death shortens not his own life."

"But is this law?" the friend asked.

"Yes, truly, it is. It is the coroner's inquest law."

"Do you want to know the truth?" the friend asked. "If she had not been a gentlewoman, she would have been buried outside of consecrated ground."

"Why, that's right," the gravedigger said. "It's the more pity that great folk should have legal approval in this world to drown or hang themselves, more than their fellow Christians. Come, give me my spade. There is no ancient gentlemen but gardeners, ditchers, and grave-makers: They hold up Adam's profession."

"Was Adam a gentleman?"

"He was the first who ever bore arms," the gravedigger said.

"Why, he had none. There is no way that Adam, the first man, ever had a coat of arms."

"What, are you a heathen?" the gravedigger asked. "How do you understand the Scripture? The Scripture says, 'Adam digged.' How could Adam dig without arms?

"I'll put another question to you: If you cannot answer it correctly, confess —"

The usual expression was "Confess and be hanged."

The friend interrupted, "— what is your question?"

"What man is he who builds stronger than the mason, the shipwright, or the carpenter?"

"The gallows-maker," the friend answered, "because the gallows outlives a thousand tenants."

"I like your wit well, truly," the gravedigger said. "The gallows is a good answer. It does well, but how does it do well? It does well to those who do ill; now you do ill to say that the gallows is built stronger than the church. *Argal*, the gallows may do well to you.

"Come on, try again. Come on."

"Who builds stronger than a mason, a shipwright, or a carpenter?"

"Yes, tell me the correct answer, and then you can knock off for the day."

"That's a good reward. I can tell you the answer now."

"Tell me."

"I don't know the answer."

Hamlet and Horatio arrived on the scene and listened to the gravedigger and his friend talk.

"Cudgel your brains no more about it, for your dull ass will not mend his pace with beating. Even if you hit its back with a stick, it will walk slowly," the gravedigger said. "But when you are asked this question next time, answer 'a gravedigger.' Why? Because the houses that he makes last until Doomsday. Go, get you to Yaughan the bartender. Fetch me a tankard of liquor."

The gravedigger's friend departed.

The gravedigger sang as he dug, punctuating the song with the grunts of working:

"*In youth, when I did love, did love,*

"*I thought it was very sweet,*

"*To contract* [grunt] *the time, for* [grunt] *my advantage,*

"*Oh, I thought, there* [grunt] *was nothing* [grunt] *meet.*"

"Has this fellow no respect for his occupation? Doesn't he realize that he is singing while he digs a grave?" Hamlet asked Horatio.

"He has grown accustomed to graves, and so he is free and easy around them," Horatio said.

"That is true," Hamlet said. "The hand that does little work is more sensitive because it is not calloused. People who do not have to work for a living can afford to be sensitive."

The Gravedigger sang these verses:

"*But age, with his stealing steps,*

"*Has clawed me in his clutch,*

"*And has shipped me back into the land,*

"*As if I had never been born.*"

The gravedigger threw a skull out of the grave he was digging.

Hamlet said, "That skull had a tongue in it, and could sing once. Look at how the knave jowls — throws — it to the ground, as if it were Cain's jawbone. Cain did the first murder: According to folk tradition, he used the jawbone of an ass to kill Abel, his brother."

Hamlet thought, *Now an ass is wielding the jawbone of Cain.*

Hamlet continued, "This skull might be the head of a politician, a schemer, whom this ass now lords over as a benefit of his office. This skull may have belonged to a schemer who would have circumvented God, might it not?"

The first schemer was Cain, who in Genesis 4:9 would not give God a straight answer: "*And the Lord said unto Cain, Where is Abel thy brother? And he said, I know not: Am I my brother's keeper?*"

"It might be, my lord," Horatio replied to Hamlet.

"Or it might be the skull of a courtier, who could once say, 'Good morning, sweet lord! How are you, good lord?' This might be the skull of my Lord Such-a-one, who praised my Lord Such-another-one's horse, when he meant to borrow it, might it not?"

"Yes, my lord."

"Why, that's right," Hamlet said. "And it might be the skull of my Lady Worm. It now lacks a lower jaw, and it is knocked about with a gravedigger's spade.

"Here's a fine alteration in fortune, a movement of the Wheel of Fortune, if we had the ability to see it. Was the cost of bringing these bones to full maturity so little that we are justified in using them in throwing games? My bones ache when I think about that."

The gravedigger sang these lines:

"*A pickaxe, and a spade, a spade,*

"*And furthermore a shrouding sheet:*

"*Oh, a pit of clay for to be made*

"*For such a guest is meet.*"

He threw another skull out of the hole he was digging.

Hamlet said, "There's another skull. That might be the skull of a lawyer. Why not? Where be his quiddities now, his quillets — his subtleties and quibbles — his cases, his tenures, and his tricks? Why does he allow this rude knave now to knock him about the hole with a dirty shovel, and will not tell him that he is bringing a lawsuit against him for the crime of battering. Ha!

"The fellow whose skull this is might have been in his time a great buyer of land, with his statutes, his recognizances, his fines, his double vouchers, his recoveries — and his all that other legal mumbo-jumbo.

"Is this the fine, aka end, of his fines, and the recovery of his recoveries, to have his fine, aka handsome, pate full of fine, aka finely ground, dirt? Will his vouchers vouch him no more of his purchases, and double ones, too, than the length and breadth of a pair of indentures? The documents for his lands will hardly lie in this box — his legal deeds will hardly fit in his grave, which is now his deed-box. He used to own all those properties, but now all he has is a grave."

"A grave, and not a jot more, my lord," Horatio said.

"Is not parchment made of sheepskins?" Hamlet asked.

"Yes, my lord, and of calfskins, too."

"Those who seek assurance in parchment are sheep and calves — they are fools."

He added, "I will speak to this fellow."

He said to the gravedigger, "Whose grave is this?"

"Mine, sir," the gravedigger answered.

He sang, "*Oh, a pit of clay for to be made*

"*For such a guest is meet.*"

"I think it is your grave, indeed," Hamlet said, "because you lie in it."

Hamlet and the gravedigger began to pun on two meanings of "lie" — "tell an untruth" versus "lie down."

"You lie out of it, sir, and therefore it is not yours," the gravedigger replied. "As for my part, I do not lie in it, and yet it is mine."

The gravedigger would not lie down permanently in the grave, but it was his grave to dig.

"You do lie in it because you are in it and you say it is yours," Hamlet said. "This grave is for the dead, not for the quick; therefore, you lie."

"It is a quick and lively lie, sir," the gravedigger said. "It will go away again — from me to you. If I am lying, then you are lying."

The gravedigger was punning on two meanings of "quick" — "be fast" versus "be alive."

"Who is the man for whom you are digging this grave?" Hamlet asked.

"I am digging it for no man, sir."

"For which woman, then?"

"For no woman, either."

"Who is to be buried in it?"

"One who was a woman, sir, but rest her soul, she's dead."

Hamlet said to Horatio, "How strict in his use of language this knave is! We must speak as carefully as if we were navigating at sea, or equivocation will undo and ruin us.

"By the Lord, Horatio, for the past three years I have taken a note of it; people nowadays have grown so refined and finicky and picky that the toe of the peasant comes so near the heel of the courtier that the peasant kicks the sore on the heel of the courtier."

Hamlet asked the gravedigger, "How long have you been a grave-maker?"

"Of all the days in the year, I came to be a gravedigger on that day that our most recent King Hamlet fought and defeated old Fortinbras."

"How long ago was that?"

"Don't you know that?" the gravedigger asked. "Every fool knows that. It was the very day that young Hamlet was born — the young Hamlet who is mad, and who was sent to England."

"Why was he sent to England?" Hamlet asked.

"Why, because he was mad: he shall recover his wits there, or if he does not, it's no great matter there."

"Why?"

"His madness will not even be noticed in England," the gravedigger said. "The men of England are as mad as Hamlet."

"How did he become mad?"

"Very strangely, they say."

"How strangely?"

"By losing his wits."

"For what reason? Upon what ground?"

"Upon what ground? Why, here in Denmark," the gravedigger replied. "I have been sexton here, man and boy, thirty years."

"How long will a man lie in the earth before he rots?"

"Assuming that he is not rotting before he dies — we have many diseased corpses nowadays that will hardly keep together before they are buried — he will last you some eight or nine years. A tanner will last you nine years."

"Why does he take longer to rot than another corpse?"

"Why, sir, his hide is so tanned with his trade, that he will keep out water a great long while," the gravedigger said. "Water is a grievous decayer of a nasty dead body."

He picked up a skull and said, "Look at this skull now; this skull has lain in the earth twenty-three years."

"Whose skull was it?" Hamlet asked.

"A whoreson mad fellow's it was," the gravedigger replied. "Whose do you think it was?"

"I don't know."

"May a pestilence fall on him because of his being a mad rogue!" the gravedigger said. "He poured a glass of Rhine wine on my head once. This same skull, sir, was the skull of Yorick, the King's jester."

"This skull?"

"Yes."

"Let me see it," Hamlet said.

The gravedigger gave Hamlet the skull.

Holding it, Hamlet said, "Alas, poor Yorick! I knew him, Horatio. He was a fellow of infinite jest, of most excellent imagination. He carried me on his back a thousand times; and now, how abhorrent in my imagination it is to realize that this is his skull! I feel ready to vomit. Here used to be those lips that I kissed I don't know how often. Where are your jokes now, Yorick? Where are your gambols? Where are your songs? Where are your flashes of merriment that used to make the people sitting at the table roar with laughter? No one is now ready to mock your own grinning? Are you quite down in the mouth?

"Now go to a lady's chamber, and tell her that although she paints on her makeup an inch thick, to this — a grinning skull — she must at last come; make her laugh at that.

"Please, Horatio, tell me something."

"What, my lord?"

"Do you think that Alexander the Great, conqueror of all the world that was known to him, looked like this when he was in the earth?"

"Yes, I am sure that he did."

"Did he smell like this? Ugh!"

Hamlet put down the skull.

"Yes, I am sure that he did, my lord."

"To what base uses we may return when we die, Horatio!" Hamlet said. Why, can't my reason trace the noble dust of Alexander from the time of his burial until it stops up a bung-hole — a hole from which liquid is poured from a cask or barrel?"

"To think that is to think too much about it."

"No, indeed, not a jot," Hamlet said. "We can trace his journey without excessive ingenuity; we can trace what is likely and reasonable. We are made of dust, and to dust we return. Alexander the Great died, Alexander was buried, Alexander returned to dust. The dust is earth; of earth we make loam, which we use to make bricks and stoppers; of that loam, whereof Alexander's dust is an ingredient, might they not make a stopper for a beer-barrel?

"Imperious Julius Caesar, dead and turned to clay, might stop a hole in a wall to keep the wind away. Oh, that that earth, which stormed the world, should patch a wall to expel the winter storm!

"But let's be quiet! Let's be quiet! Let's stand aside and out of the way. Here comes the King."

A funeral procession entered the graveyard. The procession consisted of a priest, the corpse of Ophelia, Laertes, King Claudius and Queen Gertrude, a priest, and others.

Hamlet said, "I see the Queen, the courtiers, but whose corpse is this whom they follow? And with such truncated rites? This shows that the corpse they are following did with desperate hand take its own life. Because of the mourners, I can see that the corpse was highborn.

"Let us hide here for awhile, and watch."

Hamlet and Horatio hid themselves.

Laertes asked, "What other funeral rites can be performed?"

Hamlet said to Horatio, "That is Laertes, a very noble youth. Look and listen."

Again, Laertes asked, "What other funeral rites can be performed?"

The priest replied, "I have performed her obsequies as far as I am permitted. Her death was suspicious. If not for the King's command, she would have been buried in unsanctified ground and have stayed there until the sound of the last trumpet on the Day of Judgment. Instead of charitable prayers being said over her corpse, shards of pottery, flints, and pebbles would have been thrown on her. However, she has been allowed to have her virgin's garland, flowers strewn on her maiden's grave, the bell rung as she was carried to her grave, and a few other burial rites."

"Can't anything else be done for her?" Laertes asked.

"No more can be done," the priest said. "We would profane the service of the dead if for her we were to sing a solemn Mass and do other things we do for peacefully departed souls."

"Lay her in the earth," Laertes said, "and from her fair and unpolluted flesh may violets spring! I tell you, churlish priest, that my sister shall be a ministering angel while you lie howling in Hell."

Hamlet realized whose corpse was being buried: "What, the beautiful Ophelia!"

Queen Gertrude scattered flowers and said, "Sweets to the sweet. Farewell! I hoped that you would be my Hamlet's wife. I thought that I would strew your bride-bed and not your grave with flowers, sweet maiden."

"May treble woe fall ten times treble on that cursed head whose wicked deed deprived you of your most ingenious sense," Laertes said. "Don't throw earth on her corpse just yet. Wait until I have held her once more in my arms."

He jumped into the grave and said, "Now pile your dust upon the living and dead, until you have made a mountain on this flat area — a mountain higher than old Mount Pelion, or the blue, sky-reaching head of Mount Olympus."

Hamlet came forward and said, "Who is he whose grief bears such an emphasis? Who is he whose phrases of sorrow conjures the wandering planets, and makes them stand still like wonder-wounded hearers?

"This is I: Hamlet the Dane."

By calling himself "Hamlet the Dane," Hamlet was asserting his right to the throne. "Hamlet the Dane" meant "Hamlet, rightful ruler of Denmark."

Hamlet thought that Laertes was deliberately showing excessive grief, something that Hamlet considered to be the equivalent of a rhetorician's trick.

Laertes climbed out of the grave and said to Hamlet, "May the Devil take your soul!"

Laertes began to grapple with Hamlet, who said, "You are not praying well. Please, take your fingers away from my throat. Although I am not irascible and rash, yet I have something dangerous in me that you in your wisdom ought to fear. Keep your hands off me."

King Claudius ordered his attendants, "Separate them."

Queen Gertrude said, "Hamlet, Hamlet!"

A number of people began to speak, "Gentlemen —"

Horatio said to Hamlet, "My good lord, be calm."

The attendants separated Hamlet and Laertes.

"I will fight Laertes upon this theme until my eyelids can no longer move," Hamlet said. "I will fight him until the least sign of life has left my body."

"Oh, my son, what theme do you mean?" Queen Gertrude asked.

"Love for Ophelia," Hamlet replied. "I loved Ophelia. Forty thousand brothers could not, with all their quantity of love, make up the sum of the love I felt for her."

Hamlet then said, "Laertes, what will you do for her?"

King Claudius said, "Hamlet is mad, Laertes."

"Laertes, for the love of God," Queen Gertrude said, "have patience with Hamlet."

"By God's wounds," Hamlet said to Laertes, "show me what you will do. Will you weep? Will you fight? Will you fast? Will you hurt yourself? Will you drink bitter vinegar? Will you eat a crocodile? Whatever you say that you will do, I will actually do it.

"Did you come here to whine? To outdo my love for Ophelia by leaping in her grave? If you will be buried alive with her, then so will I. And, if you prate about mountains, let them throw millions of acres on us, until our ground, singeing its top against the burning Sun, makes Mount Ossa look like a wart! If you rant with your mouth, I'll rant as well as you."

"This is a display of Hamlet's madness," Queen Gertrude said. "And thus for awhile the fit will work on him, but soon he will droop and be silent. He will be as patient as the female dove when her nestlings, covered with golden-yellow down, hatch out of their eggs."

Hamlet said to Laertes, "Sir, listen to me. What is the reason that you are treating me this way? I have always respected you. But it does not matter. No matter how hard he tries, even Hercules can't keep cats from meowing — and the dog will have its day."

Hamlet exited.

King Claudius said, "Please, Horatio, go with him and look after him."

Horatio followed Hamlet.

King Claudius said quietly to Laertes so that Queen Gertrude did not hear, "Strengthen your patience by remembering what we talked about last night. We will put our plan into action quickly. Ophelia's grave shall have a long-lasting monument. We will have an hour of quiet, and then we will put our plan into action. Until then, be patient."

131

Hamlet and Horatio talked together in a hall in the castle.

"So much for that," Hamlet said. "Now let me tell you the other part of my story. Do you remember the background?"

"I remember, my lord," Horatio replied.

"Sir, in my heart, while I was on the ship sailing to England, there was a kind of fighting that would not let me sleep. I thought that I lay more uncomfortably than failed mutineers in fetters. I then acted rashly — and let me praise rashness because rash actions sometimes serve us well when our carefully planned plots falter. That should teach us that a divinity shapes what happens to us although we ineffectually and roughly try to shape what happens to us."

"That is most certain and true," Horatio replied.

"Rashly, I got up from my cabin, with my long sea-coat wrapped about me. In the dark I groped to find Rosencrantz and Guildenstern. I found them, and I took the letter that King Claudius had given to them to give to the King of England. Finally, I withdrew to my own room again, where I made so bold — my fears making me forget my manners — to unseal the letter, which was their grand commission.

"Written in the letter I found, Horatio — oh, royal knavery! — an exact command, garnished with many different sorts of reasons about what is good for the King of Denmark and what is good for the King of England, too, with a description of the danger I would be if I remained alive, that the King of England, as soon as he had read this letter should without delay — even a delay to sharpen the axe — cut off my head."

"Unbelievable!" Horatio said.

"Here's the letter itself," Hamlet replied, handing Horatio the document. "Read it when you have time. Do you want to know what I did?"

"Yes, please."

"Being thus surrounded with villainies to ensnare me and before I could even begin to consciously think about it, my brain leapt into action — I sat down, thought up a new commission that would supposedly come from King Claudius, and wrote it in an official hand — bureaucrats have to have good handwriting. I used to think, as our statesmen do, that it was base and beneath me to have good handwriting. I even wanted to unlearn what I had learned. But, sir, good handwriting now did me good service. I also imitated the flowery language that King Claudius used in the letter. My forgery of an official letter was quite good. Do you want to know what I wrote?"

"Yes, my good lord."

"I wrote an earnest command from King Claudius to the King of England. I wrote that as the King of England was his faithful tributary, as love and friendship ought to flourish between them like the palm tree, as peace ought to come with rural prosperity, and as peace ought to join them in friendship like a comma joins two parts of a sentence, and I wrote many other 'as'es of great charge — or asses carrying a great burden. The commandment was that the bearers of the letter ought to be put to death immediately — without first being given time to go to a priest for confession, penance, and absolution."

"Official letters have official seals," Horatio said. "How did you seal this letter?"

"Why, even in that was Heaven provident," Hamlet replied. "I had my father's signet ring in my possession; it was a replica of that Danish seal. I folded up the letter the same way as the original letter, signed it with the name of King Claudius, used my father's signet ring to form an impression on the wax that sealed the letter, and replaced it safely. Rosencrantz and Guildenstern did not realize that the letter had been replaced.

"The following day, pirates attacked us, and you know what happened after that."

"So Guildenstern and Rosencrantz go to their deaths," Horatio said.

"Why, man, they made love to this employment given to them by King Claudius," Hamlet said. "They were eager to serve him and carry out his orders. Their deaths will not disturb my conscience; their deaths will occur because of their own actions. It is dangerous for the baser sort of people to come in between the thrusts of dangerous rapiers wielded by angry and powerful enemies."

"Why, what a King is this Claudius!" Horatio said.

"Claudius has killed my father the King and whored my mother, he came in between me and the circle of nobles who selected the next King and thus dashed my hope to be King, he has tried to get me killed with trickery despite our being kin. Don't you think I have a right to take action? Wouldn't it be perfect if I were to get revenge against him? Wouldn't it be damnable to allow this canker — this cancer, this malignant sore — of our human nature to commit further evil?"

"King Claudius will soon learn what has happened in England. He will learn that Rosencrantz and Guildenstern are dead," Horatio said.

"He will learn that soon, but I can act quickly," Hamlet replied. "A man's life's is so short that he can do no more than to say 'One' before he dies. But I am very sorry, good Horatio, that I forgot myself when I saw Laertes. I should not have spoken to him the way I did. He and I are suffering the same kind of grief. By looking at the reflection of my cause, I see the portrait of his."

Both Hamlet and Laertes were mourning the death of Ophelia, and both were mourning the death of their fathers. In Laertes' case, however, it was Hamlet who had killed his father.

Hamlet continued, "I'll court Laertes' favor and try to be friends with him. But the passionate expression of his grief over Ophelia's death certainly put me into a towering passion and anger."

Horatio said, "I hear someone. Who is coming here?"

Osric, a foolish courtier, entered the room.

Osric took off his hat to show respect to Hamlet, who was higher in society than he was.

"Your lordship is very welcome back to Denmark," Osric said to Hamlet.

"I humbly thank you, sir," Hamlet replied.

Hamlet, who had little or no respect for Osric, asked Horatio, "Do you know this mosquito?"

"No, my good lord."

"You are lucky, because it is unfortunate to know him," Hamlet said. "He has much land, and it is fertile. Let a beast be the lord of beasts, and a plate for him shall be put on the King's dining table. This man is a chatterer, but as I say, he enjoys the possession of a large quantity of dirt."

"Sweet lord, if your lordship is at leisure, I would like to impart a thing to you from his majesty," Osric said.

"I will receive it, sir, with all diligence of spirit," Hamlet said.

Osric was using fancy language, and so Hamlet was using fancy language as a form of mockery.

Hamlet added, "You have already shown courtesy to me by taking off your hat. That is enough courtesy. You may put your hat on your head again."

Osric, who was a stickler for the rules of etiquette, replied, "I thank your lordship, but it is very hot."

This was an excuse for him not to put on his hat in front of Prince Hamlet.

"No, believe me, it is very cold," Hamlet said. "The wind is blowing from the north."

"It is rather cold, my lord, indeed," Osric said.

"But yet I think that it is very sultry and hot for my temperament," Hamlet said.

"Exceedingly, my lord," Osric replied. "It is very sultry, as it were — I cannot tell how. But, my lord, his majesty asked me to tell you that he has laid a great wager on your head. Sir, this is the message —"

"Please," Hamlet said. He motioned for Osric to put on his hat.

"No, my good lord," Osric said. "I am more comfortable like this, believe me."

He added, "Sir, Laertes is newly come to court. Believe me, he is a perfect gentleman, full of most excellent distinguishing characteristics, of very pleasing manners and handsome appearance. Indeed, to speak justly of him, he is the model of gentlemanly behavior, for you shall find in him the container of whatever parts a gentleman would want to see in another gentleman."

Hamlet continued to satirize Osric's elevated language: "Sir, Laertes suffers no loss when you describe him, although, I know, to mention each item in his inventory of good qualities would dizzy the arithmetic of memory, and still lag behind because of his many excellences. But, in the truth of extolling his great qualities, I take him to be a soul of greatness. His infusion of such rare excellences is such that, to speak true diction of him, his only equal is the image in his mirror; and whoever would try to match him would be only his shadow, nothing more."

"Your lordship speaks most infallibly of him," Osric said.

"What is the concernancy, sir?" Hamlet said. "Why does this concern us? Why do we wrap the gentleman with our gasping breath — breath that gasps with admiration for him?"

"Sir?" Osric asked.

"Isn't it possible to speak in another tongue?" Horatio asked. "Can't you two use a simpler language? Not even Osric can understand this language. Eventually, you will have to use simpler language."

Hamlet continued to use fancy language: "What imports the nomination — the naming — of this gentleman?"

"Of Laertes?"

"Osric's purse is empty already," Horatio said. "All his golden words are spent."

"Yes, I mean him, sir," Hamlet said.

"I know you are not ignorant —" Osric started to say.

"I wish you did know that I am not ignorant, sir," Hamlet interrupted, "but yet, truly, if you did know that I am not ignorant, it still would not give me much credit. Well, sir?"

Osric tried to continue: "You are not ignorant of Laertes' excellence —"

Hamlet interrupted, "I dare not confess that I know his excellence, lest I should be thought to be saying that I share his excellence. In order for me truly to understand his excellence, I would have to possess and demonstrate that I possess that excellence."

"I mean, sir, Laertes' excellence with his weapons," Osric said. "In the opinion of people who are in his service, he is unequalled in excellence with them."

"What's his weapon?" Hamlet asked.

"Rapier and dagger," Osric replied.

"That's two of his weapons, but that is fine," Hamlet said.

"King Claudius, sir, has wagered six Barbary horses that you can defeat Laertes, who has in turn impawned six French rapiers and daggers, with their accessories, including belts, straps attaching the sword to the belt, and so on. Three of the carriages, truly, are very well designed, very appropriate for the hilts, very finely wrought carriages, and very richly decorated."

"What do you mean by the word 'carriages'?" Hamlet asked.

"I knew that you would need explanatory notes in the margins — or footnotes or endnotes — before you were done talking to him," Horatio said to Hamlet.

"The carriages, sir, are the hangers," Osric said.

Osric was mistaken. Hangers were the straps attaching the sword to the belt. Carriages were wheeled structures used to transport cannon.

"The word would be more appropriate if we could carry cannon by our sides instead of swords," Hamlet said. "Until then, I prefer that we continue to use the word 'hangers.'

"But let us move on. King Claudius has bet six Barbary horses, and Laertes has bet six French swords and their accessories, including three richly decorated 'carriages.' The things wagered show it is Denmark versus France.

"But what is this wager about? Why is this stuff — 'impawned,' you call it — being wagered?"

"King Claudius, sir, has bet that in a dozen bouts between yourself and Laertes, Laertes shall not defeat you by three bouts. Whoever touches the other with their blunted rapier will get a hit and win that bout. If Laertes wins eight bouts, he wins the bet; if you win five bouts, you win the bet for King Claudius. The bouts can begin right away if you vouchsafe — give me — your answer."

"What if I answer 'no'?" Hamlet asked.

"I mean, my lord, if you vouchsafe the opposition of your person in trial," Osric said.

"Sir, I will walk here in the hall," Hamlet replied. "If it pleases his majesty, it is the time of day for exercise with me. Let the foils — the rapiers — be brought, if the gentleman Laertes is willing, and if King Claudius wants the fencing match to proceed. I will win the fencing match for King Claudius if I can; if I cannot, I will gain nothing but my shame and the hits that Laertes will give me."

"Should I give this answer to the King?" Osric asked.

"Yes, sir," Hamlet said. "Add to it whatever rhetorical flourishes you wish to add."

"I commend my duty to your lordship," Osric said.

The verb "commend" can mean either "present, aka offer" or "praise." Osric meant he was presenting his duty to Hamlet — a fancy way of saying that he would run the errand for Hamlet.

"Yours," Hamlet replied. This was a dismissal.

Osric put his hat on his head and left to run the errand.

Hamlet said to Horatio, "He does well to commend — to praise — his duty himself; no one else would praise it for him."

"This young lapwing runs away with the eggshell on his head," Horatio said.

Lapwings were proverbially young and stupid birds. They left the nest quickly after hatching from their eggs — so quickly that it was as if they still had a piece of the eggshell on top of their head.

Hamlet said about Osric's excessive sense of etiquette and formality, "He used to bow courteously to his mother's nipple, before he sucked it.

"This drossy age — this shoddy age with no sense of real nobility — dotes on Osric and many more of the same company, but they have only got the tune of the time and the outward habit of encounter. They look the part of a courtier, and they can make some of the sounds of a courtier, but they have no substance. They have a kind of yeasty collection of rhetorical tricks that helps them mingle with — and impose on — men of very carefully considered and winnowed opinions. If all you do is blow on Osric and others like him, you blow away the bubbles and nothing remains."

A lord entered the hall and said, "My lord, his majesty sent his compliments to you by young Osric, who brings back to him the news that you will attend him in the hall. He sent me to ask you if your pleasure is still to fence now with Laertes, or if you want to fence later."

"I am constant to my purpose," Hamlet said. "I will do whatever pleases the King. If he wants me to fence now, I am ready. If he wants me to fence later, I will fence later. Now or later are both fine, as long as I am as fit and ready to fence as I am now."

"The King and Queen and all the others will come down to the hall now," the lord said.

"In happy time," Hamlet said. "Now is as good a time as any."

"The Queen wants you to be courteous to Laertes before you begin to fence," the lord said.

"She well instructs me," Hamlet said. "I will do as she wishes."

The Lord exited from the hall.

Horatio said, "You will lose this wager, my lord."

"I do not think so," Hamlet replied. "Ever since Laertes went to France, I have been continually practicing fencing. I shall win at the odds given — Laertes has been given a handicap. You cannot imagine how ill I feel here in my heart, but that does not matter."

"My good lord —" Horatio began to say.

"It is only foolishness," Hamlet interrupted. "It is such a kind of misgiving, such as would perhaps trouble a woman."

"If your mind feels uneasy, listen to it," Horatio replied. "I will stop them from coming here, and I will tell them that you are not ready to fence."

"No," Hamlet said. "We defy omens and the interpretation of omens. There's a special providence in the fall of a sparrow."

Hamlet was thinking of the Bible. Matthew 10:29-31 recounts the words of Jesus when he was reassuring his disciples, "*Are not two sparrows sold for a farthing? and one of them shall not fall on the ground without your Father. But the very hairs of your head are all numbered. Fear ye not therefore, ye are of more value than many sparrows.*"

Hamlet continued, "If death comes now, death will not come later. If death does not come later, death will come now. If death does not come now, then death must come later. The readiness is all. Since no man knows anything about what he leaves, what does it matter if he dies now?"

Again, Hamlet was thinking of the Bible. Matthew 24:44 states, "*Therefore be ye also ready: for in such an hour as ye think not the Son of man cometh.*" We must always be ready for death. And since we do not know what we leave behind, we ought not to fear an early death. An early death may stop us from having a long and wretched life.

Hamlet heard a noise and said, "But let's say no more."

King Claudius, Queen Gertrude, Laertes, some lords, Osric, and some attendants entered the hall. The attendants brought such items as rapiers.

"Come, Hamlet, come, and take this hand from me," King Claudius, who was holding Laertes' hand, said.

King Claudius put Laertes' hand into Hamlet's hand.

Hamlet said politely to Laertes, "Give me your pardon, sir; I've done you wrong. But pardon it, as you are a gentleman. This presence — this assembly of people — knows, and you must have heard, how I am punished with sore distraction — severe mental distress. What I have done that might roughly awake your natural filial feelings, honor, and disapproval, I here proclaim was done due to my madness.

"Was it Hamlet who wronged Laertes? Never was it Hamlet. If Hamlet is taken away from himself, and when he is not himself he does wrong Laertes, then Hamlet does not do it — Hamlet denies doing it. Hamlet is not responsible for his action.

"Who does it, then? His madness. If this is true, then Hamlet is one of the people who are wronged. His own madness is poor Hamlet's enemy.

"Sir, in front of this audience, I proclaim my innocence and I disavow all intended and intentional evil. Let this free me so far in your most generous thoughts — believe that I have shot my arrow over the house, and hurt my brother. I have not done anything with the intention to hurt you."

How are Hamlet and Laertes like brothers? They both loved Ophelia, and they both suffered the death of Ophelia and the killing of their father.

Laertes replied, "I am satisfied so far as natural feeling goes, although the deaths of my father and my sister ought to drive me to seek revenge — but I am not satisfied so far as my honor is concerned. I will not be reconciled with you until some elder masters, of known honor, give me a statement based on precedent that favors peace and reconciliation and will keep my name and reputation unsullied. But until that time, I accept your offered friendship as friendship, and I will not wrong or spurn it."

Despite his words, Laertes was still planning to kill Hamlet in the fencing contest.

"I am grateful that you accept my offered friendship," Hamlet said. "And I will frankly and freely participate in this wager between brothers."

He said to the attendants, "Give us the foils — the rapiers."

"Give me a foil," Laertes said.

"I'll be your foil, Laertes," Hamlet said. "Against the background of my ignorance of fencing, your skill shall, like a star in the darkest night, stick out as fiery indeed."

Hamlet was punning on the word "foil." One meaning of "foil" was "rapier"; another was "setting for a rich gem." The foil was designed to show off the rich gem to best advantage.

"You mock me, sir," Laertes said.

"No, I swear it by this hand," Hamlet said, holding up a hand.

"Give them the foils, young Osric," King Claudius said.

He added, "Kinsman Hamlet, do you know the wager?"

"Very well, my lord," Hamlet said. "Your grace has wagered on the weaker side."

"I do not fear betting on you to win," King Claudius replied. "I have seen you both fence. But since Laertes is better, we therefore have odds. Laertes has a handicap."

Laertes said, "This rapier is too heavy; let me see another."

He was being careful to get the rapier whose point was not blunted and to whose point poison had been applied.

"I like this rapier well," Hamlet said. "These foils are all the same length?"

"Yes, my good lord," Osric answered.

A fencer with a longer rapier than the other fencer would have an unfair advantage.

"Set the flagons of wine upon that table," King Claudius ordered. "If Hamlet gives the first or second hit, or after having lost the first two bouts wins the third bout, let all the battlements their cannon fire. The King shall drink to Hamlet's better breath and enhanced vigor, and he will throw a union in the cup of wine. This union shall be richer than any that four successive Kings of Denmark have worn in their crown."

A union is a very valuable pearl, one valuable enough to be worn in the crown of a King. The wine would dissolve the pearl, something that was supposed to honor Hamlet, who would drink the wine.

King Claudius continued, "Give me the cups. And let the kettledrum speak to the trumpet, and the trumpet speak to the cannoneers outside, and the cannons speak to the Heavens, and the Heavens speak to the Earth, and let them all say, 'Now the King drinks to Hamlet.'

"Come, begin the fencing contest. You judges, keep a close eye on the contest."

"Come on, sir," Hamlet said to Laertes.

"Come on, my lord," Laertes replied.

They fenced.

"One," Hamlet said. "I have hit you. I have touched you with the point of my rapier."

"No," Laertes said.

"Judgment," Hamlet requested of the judges.

"A hit, a very palpable hit," Osric said.

"Well, so be it," Laertes said. "Let us fence again."

"Wait," King Claudius said. "Give me a drink. Hamlet, this pearl is yours. Here's to your health."

King Claudius drank, and kettledrums and trumpets sounded and the cannons fired.

King Claudius put the pearl and some poison in a cup of wine and said, "Give Hamlet the cup."

"I'll play this bout first," Hamlet said. "Set the cup of wine aside for awhile."

He said to Laertes, "Come on."

They fenced, and Hamlet said, "Another hit; what do you say?"

"A touch, a touch, I do confess it," Laertes replied.

"Our son shall win," King Claudius said.

"He's sweaty, and out of breath," Queen Gertrude said. "Here, Hamlet, take my handkerchief and rub your brows. The Queen drinks to your fortune, Hamlet."

She picked up the cup of poisoned wine.

"Good madam," Hamlet saluted her.

"Gertrude, do not drink," King Claudius said.

"I will, my lord," Queen Gertrude said. "Please, pardon me."

She drank.

King Claudius thought, *It is the poisoned cup: it is too late to save her life.*

Hamlet said to his mother, "I dare not drink yet, madam, but I will by and by."

"Come, let me wipe your face," she said.

"My lord, I'll get a hit against him now," Laertes said.

"I do not think so," the King replied.

Hamlet's skill in fencing had impressed Laertes, who thought, *And yet it almost goes against my conscience to kill him.*

To use poison in what was supported to be a friendly fencing contest was a violation of honor, as was using an unblunted rapier against an opponent who was using a blunt rapier.

"Come on, let us fight the third bout, Laertes," Hamlet said. "You are only dallying, not fencing. Please, make your thrust with the utmost force that you can. I am afraid that you are treating me as if I were a child."

"Do you think that?" Laertes said. "Come on and fence!"

They fenced.

"Nothing, either way," Osric said. "No hits scored."

"Have at you now!" Laertes said.

They fenced, and Laertes wounded Hamlet. They wrestled, dropped their rapiers, and picked up each other's rapier. Hamlet now had the poisoned rapier.

"Part them; they are incensed," King Claudius ordered.

"No," Hamlet said.

He said to Laertes, "Come, let us fence again."

They fenced, and Hamlet wounded Laertes.

Queen Gertrude fell.

"Look after the Queen!" Osric shouted. "Stop the fencing!"

"Both Hamlet and Laertes are bleeding," Horatio said. "The points of their rapiers ought to have been blunted."

He asked Hamlet, "How are you, my lord?"

Osric asked Laertes, "How are you, my lord?"

Laertes replied, "Why, I am like a famously foolish woodcock captured in my own trap, Osric. I am justly killed because of my own treachery."

"How is the Queen?" Hamlet asked.

"She fainted when she saw them bleed," King Claudius said.

"No, no, the drink, the drink — oh, my dear Hamlet — the drink, the drink! I am poisoned," Queen Gertrude said.

She died.

"Villainy!" Hamlet shouted. "Lock the door! Treachery! Find the source of the treachery!"

"It is here, Hamlet," Laertes said. "Hamlet, you are slain. No medicine in the world can do you any good. You have not half an hour of life left. The treacherous instrument is in your hand; its sharp point has been dipped in poison. The foul trickery has turned itself on me. Here I lie, never to rise again. Your mother has been poisoned. I will live no more. The King — the King's to blame."

"The sharp point of this rapier!" Hamlet said. "Dipped in poison, too! Then, venom, do your work."

Hamlet stabbed King Claudius.

People shouted, "Treason! Treason!"

"Defend me, friends," King Claudius pleaded. "I am only wounded."

"Here, you incestuous, murderous, damned Dane, drink the rest of this poisoned potion."

Hamlet forced King Claudius to drink the poison.

As King Claudius died, Hamlet said to him, "Is your union here? Follow my mother."

Even now Hamlet was able to pun. "Union" meant both "valuable pearl" and "marriage between King Claudius and Queen Gertrude."

"He is justly served," Laertes said. "It is a poison he himself mixed. Exchange forgiveness with me, noble Hamlet. My death and my father's death will not fall upon you, and your death will not fall on me. We will forgive each other."

"May Heaven absolve you of blame!" Hamlet said. "I follow you. I am dead, Horatio. Wretched Queen, *adieu*!

"Those of you who look pale and tremble at this mischance, who are only mutes or audience to this act, if I only had time — this fell sergeant, death, is strict in his arrest and will not give me time — I could tell you ... but let it be.

"Horatio, I am dead, but you live. To those who do not know, tell them about me and my reasons for acting the way I have."

"No," Horatio said. "Don't believe that I will do that. I am more an ancient Roman than a Dane. I am willing to commit suicide. There is still some poisoned wine left in the cup."

Horatio picked up the cup, but Hamlet grabbed his arms and said, "As you are a man, give me the cup. Let go — by Heaven, I will have it."

He wrestled the cup away from Horatio and said, "Good Horatio, I shall leave a badly wounded reputation behind me unless people understand why I acted the way I have acted. If you have ever regarded me as a friend in your heart, absent you from happiness for awhile — stay out of Paradise for awhile — and in this harsh world draw your breath in pain. That way, you can tell other people my story."

The sound of marching soldiers and the sound of firing cannons were heard.

Hamlet asked, "What warlike noise is this?"

Osric came back from the door and said, "Young Fortinbras, coming victorious from Poland, gives this warlike volley to salute the also newly arrived ambassadors from England."

"I am dying, Horatio," Hamlet said. "The potent poison quite conquers my spirit. I will not live to hear the news from England. But I do prophesy that the nobles will select Fortinbras to be the next King of Denmark. He has my dying voice and recommendation; I want him to succeed me. So tell him my story, as I have urged you, with all its occurrences, greater and lesser."

He paused and then said, "The rest is silence."

He gave a long sigh and died.

"Now stops a noble heart," Horatio said. "Good night, sweet Prince, and may flights of angels sing you to your rest!"

Drums sounded, and Horatio asked, "Why are the drums coming toward us?"

Young Fortinbras, the English ambassadors, and others entered the hall.

"Where is what I have come to see?" Fortinbras said.

"What is it you want to see?" Horatio replied. "If you want to see sights of woe or wonder, sorrow or disaster, cease your search."

Fortinbras looked at all the dead bodies and said, "This quarry cries on havoc."

The word "quarry" was a hunting term that meant "a heap of slain animals." "To cry on havoc" meant "to loudly proclaim great slaughter."

Fortinbras continued, "Proud death, what feast is being prepared in your eternal cell, that you so many Princes at a shot so bloodily have struck down?"

An English ambassador said, "This sight is dismal; and our news from England has come too late. The ears — those of King Claudius — are senseless that should have listened to our news. We came here to tell him that his commandment has been fulfilled — Rosencrantz and Guildenstern are dead. From whom should we now have our thanks?"

"Not from King Claudius' mouth, even if he were alive to thank you," Horatio said. "He never gave the order for their death.

"But since you, Fortinbras, who have come from the war in Poland, and you, ambassadors from England, have all here arrived opportunely at this bloody time, please give orders that these bodies be placed high on a platform so that people can view them, and let me speak to the yet unknowing world and say how these things came about.

"You shall hear about carnal, bloody, and unnatural acts, about divine justice administered by what seem to be accidents, about slaughters due to chance, about deaths instigated by cunning and foul means, and, in this upshot, about purposes mistook that fell back on their inventors' heads.

"I can tell you about all of these things."

"Let us make haste to hear what you have to say," Fortinbras said. "We will call the noblest people to be in the audience.

"As for me, with sorrow I embrace my fortune. I have some still-remembered rights in this Kingdom, and now circumstances allow me to claim my rights. I have some claim to be the King of Denmark."

"Of that I shall also have cause to speak," Horatio said. "And I will talk about the words that Hamlet said as he lay dying; he gave you his voice and recommendation, and those will encourage other nobles to make you King.

"But let what I have recommended be immediately done. Men's minds are wild because they do not know Hamlet's story. More misfortunes may happen unless we stop plots and correct errors."

"Let four Captains bear Hamlet, like a soldier, to the platform," Fortinbras said. "Hamlet was likely, had he been put on the throne, to have proved to be most royal. To mark his passing, soldiers' music and the rites of war — such as saluting him with a volley of shots — will speak loudly for him.

"Take up the bodies. Such a sight as this becomes a battlefield, but here it is much amiss.

"Go, order the soldiers to shoot a volley of shots to honor Hamlet."

Marching music sounded. They carried away the bodies, and a salute of gunshots sounded.

AFTERWORD

A question: According to Hamlet's own beliefs, will he end up in Heaven or in Hell?

Appendix A: About the Author

It was a dark and stormy night. Suddenly a cry rang out, and on a hot summer night in 1954, Josephine, wife of Carl Bruce, gave birth to a boy — me. Unfortunately, this young married couple allowed Reuben Saturday, Josephine's brother, to name their first-born. Reuben, aka "The Joker," decided that Bruce was a nice name, so he decided to name me Bruce Bruce. I have gone by my middle name — David — ever since.

Being named Bruce David Bruce hasn't been all bad. Bank tellers remember me very quickly, so I don't often have to show an ID. It can be fun in charades, also. When I was a counselor as a teenager at Camp Echoing Hills in Warsaw, Ohio, a fellow counselor gave the signs for "sounds like" and "two words," then she pointed to a bruise on her leg twice. Bruise Bruise? Oh yeah, Bruce Bruce is the answer!

Uncle Reuben, by the way, gave me a haircut when I was in kindergarten. He cut my hair short and shaved a small bald spot on the back of my head. My mother wouldn't let me go to school until the bald spot grew out again.

Of all my brothers and sisters (six in all), I am the only transplant to Athens, Ohio. I was born in Newark, Ohio, and have lived all around Southeastern Ohio. However, I moved to Athens to go to Ohio University and have never left.

At Ohio U, I never could make up my mind whether to major in English or Philosophy, so I got a bachelor's degree with a double major in both areas, then I added a master's degree in English and a master's degree in Philosophy. Yes, I have my MAMA degree.

Currently, and for a long time to come (I eat fruits and veggies), I am spending my retirement writing books such as *Nadia Comaneci: Perfect 10*, *The Funniest People in Dance*, *Homer's* Iliad: *A Retelling in Prose*, and *William Shakespeare's* Othello: *A Retelling in Prose*.

By the way, my sister Brenda Kennedy writes romances such as *A New Beginning* and *Shattered Dreams*.

Appendix B: Some Books by David Bruce

Retellings of a Classic Work of Literature

Arden of Faversham: *A Retelling*

Ben Jonson's The Alchemist: *A Retelling*

Ben Jonson's The Arraignment, or Poetaster: *A Retelling*

Ben Jonson's Bartholomew Fair: *A Retelling*

Ben Jonson's The Case is Altered: *A Retelling*

Ben Jonson's Catiline's Conspiracy: *A Retelling*

Ben Jonson's The Devil is an Ass: *A Retelling*

Ben Jonson's Epicene: *A Retelling*

Ben Jonson's Every Man in His Humor: *A Retelling*

Ben Jonson's Every Man Out of His Humor: *A Retelling*

Ben Jonson's The Fountain of Self-Love, or Cynthia's Revels: *A Retelling*

Ben Jonson's The Magnetic Lady, or Humors Reconciled: *A Retelling*

Ben Jonson's The New Inn, or The Light Heart: *A Retelling*

Ben Jonson's Sejanus' Fall: *A Retelling*

Ben Jonson's The Staple of News: *A Retelling*

Ben Jonson's A Tale of a Tub: *A Retelling*

Ben Jonson's Volpone, or the Fox: *A Retelling*

Christopher Marlowe's Complete Plays: Retellings

Christopher Marlowe's Dido, Queen of Carthage: *A Retelling*

Christopher Marlowe's Doctor Faustus: *Retellings of the 1604 A-Text and of the 1616 B-Text*

Christopher Marlowe's Edward II: *A Retelling*

Christopher Marlowe's The Massacre at Paris: *A Retelling*

Christopher Marlowe's The Rich Jew of Malta: *A Retelling*

Christopher Marlowe's Tamburlaine, Parts 1 and 2: *Retellings*

Dante's Divine Comedy: *A Retelling in Prose*

Dante's Inferno: *A Retelling in Prose*

Dante's Purgatory: *A Retelling in Prose*

Dante's Paradise: *A Retelling in Prose*

The Famous Victories of Henry V: *A Retelling*

From the Iliad *to the* Odyssey: *A Retelling in Prose of Quintus of Smyrna's* Posthomerica

George Chapman, Ben Jonson, and John Marston's Eastward Ho! *A Retelling*

George Peele's The Arraignment of Paris: *A Retelling*

George Peele's The Battle of Alcazar: *A Retelling*

George Peele's David and Bathsheba, and the Tragedy of Absalom: *A Retelling*

George Peele's Edward I: *A Retelling*

George Peele's The Old Wives' Tale: *A Retelling*

George-a-Greene: *A Retelling*

William Shakespeare's 1 Henry IV, aka Henry IV, Part 1: *A Retelling in Prose*

William Shakespeare's 2 Henry IV, aka Henry IV, Part 2: *A Retelling in Prose*

William Shakespeare's 1 Henry VI, aka Henry VI, Part 1: *A Retelling in Prose*

William Shakespeare's 2 Henry VI, aka Henry VI, Part 2: *A Retelling in Prose*

William Shakespeare's 3 Henry VI, aka Henry VI, Part 3: *A Retelling in Prose*

William Shakespeare's All's Well that Ends Well: *A Retelling in Prose*

William Shakespeare's Antony and Cleopatra: *A Retelling in Prose*

William Shakespeare's As You Like It: *A Retelling in Prose*

William Shakespeare's The Comedy of Errors: *A Retelling in Prose*

William Shakespeare's Coriolanus: *A Retelling in Prose*

William Shakespeare's Cymbeline: *A Retelling in Prose*

William Shakespeare's Hamlet: *A Retelling in Prose*

William Shakespeare's Henry V: *A Retelling in Prose*

William Shakespeare's Henry VIII: *A Retelling in Prose*

William Shakespeare's Julius Caesar: *A Retelling in Prose*

William Shakespeare's King John: *A Retelling in Prose*

William Shakespeare's King Lear: *A Retelling in Prose*

William Shakespeare's Love's Labor's Lost: *A Retelling in Prose*

William Shakespeare's Macbeth: *A Retelling in Prose*

William Shakespeare's Measure for Measure: *A Retelling in Prose*

William Shakespeare's The Merchant of Venice: *A Retelling in Prose*

William Shakespeare's The Merry Wives of Windsor: *A Retelling in Prose*

William Shakespeare's A Midsummer Night's Dream: *A Retelling in Prose*

William Shakespeare's Much Ado About Nothing: *A Retelling in Prose*

William Shakespeare's Othello: *A Retelling in Prose*

William Shakespeare's Pericles, Prince of Tyre: *A Retelling in Prose*

William Shakespeare's Richard II: *A Retelling in Prose*

William Shakespeare's Richard III: *A Retelling in Prose*

William Shakespeare's Romeo and Juliet: *A Retelling in Prose*

William Shakespeare's The Taming of the Shrew: *A Retelling in Prose*

William Shakespeare's The Tempest: *A Retelling in Prose*

William Shakespeare's Timon of Athens: *A Retelling in Prose*

William Shakespeare's Titus Andronicus: *A Retelling in Prose*

William Shakespeare's Troilus and Cressida: *A Retelling in Prose*

William Shakespeare's Twelfth Night: *A Retelling in Prose*

William Shakespeare's The Two Gentlemen of Verona: *A Retelling in Prose*

William Shakespeare's The Two Noble Kinsmen: *A Retelling in Prose*

William Shakespeare's The Winter's Tale: *A Retelling in Prose*